Three on one, and the odds are just right . . .

They came for him, all three at once, the one on the right the closest.

Carter caught him flush in the face with the bottle and rolled away from a roundhouse right thrown from his left. Just as Carter hit the ground the baseball bat came down across his back. He was already rolling so when it hit it wasn't a killing blow.

Carter made it to his feet with Number One coming on strong, his big paws opening and closing in anticipation.

One hand went for Carter's throat. It was a decoy. When the Killmaster went for the huge fist, the other hand crashed into his ribs.

He knew something was broken or cracked even as he smashed back into the car . . . Carter nailed him two good ones in the kneecap with his right boot and brought both fists into his face.

NICK CARTER IS IT!

"Nick Carter out-Bonds James Bond."
                            —*Buffalo Evening News*

"Nick Carter is America's #1 espionage agent."
                            —*Variety*

"Nick Carter is razor-sharp suspense."
                            —*King Features*

"Nick Carter has attracted an army of addicted readers...the books are fast, have plenty of action and just the right degree of sex...Nick Carter is the American James Bond, suave, sophisticated, a killer with both the ladies and the enemy."
                            —*The New York Times*

FROM THE NICK CARTER
KILLMASTER SERIES

THE ANDROPOV FILE

KILL MASTER

NICK CARTER

JOVE BOOKS, NEW YORK

KILLMASTER #233: THE ANDROPOV FILE

A Jove Book/published by arrangement with
The Condé Nast Publications, Inc.

PRINTING HISTORY
Jove edition/January 1988

ISBN: 0-515-09376-9

Jove Books are published by The Berkley Publishing Group,
200 Madison Avenue, New York, New York 10016.
The name "JOVE" and the "J" logo
are trademarks belonging to Jove Publications, Inc.

PRINTED IN THE UNITED STATES OF AMERICA

10 9 8 7 6 5 4 3 2 1

*Dedicated to the men of the
Secret Services of the
United States of America*

THE ANDROPOV
FILE

ONE

Moscow, February 1984

From the window of her apartment on Leninsky Prospekt, Angelina Galadin gazed out through the semidarkness at early-morning Moscow. Snow had been falling all night and it was still coming down in tiny, shimmering flakes.

Shivering, Angelina wrapped her robe more tightly around her and narrowed her eyes. Fourteen blocks away she could barely see the two massive, ornate, semicircular buildings that rose like monoliths. One of those housed the wire service where Angelina worked. And, on that morning, as she had every morning for the past two years, she would have to walk to work.

But only for a few more weeks. Then she would

1

return to the warmth of her beloved Spain. She had enjoyed her years in Moscow as cultural affairs editor for the service, but she was going to enjoy being a wife and mother more.

Still shivering, she entered the tiny bath and showered. Finished, she took a terry-cloth robe and dried her long, taut body. As she did so, her gaze wandered to the full-length mirror on the door and she giggled with delight. She hadn't yet told Luis that she was pregnant; it had only been confirmed a few weeks earlier and she'd decided she would wait until she saw him. She wanted to see his face when she told him: such announcements should not be made on the telephone, she felt.

She hoped a six-month baby would not be too embarrassing to her small-town, conservative, religious parents. She was sure her fiancé would be ecstatic at the news and they would be married as soon as she returned home.

At that moment, Angelina Galadin was the happiest woman in the world.

How could this beautiful, dark-haired Spanish woman from the village of Cordona possibly suspect that in two hours she would be dead?

Even as big and as powerful as the black Chaika limousine was, the chauffeur had trouble navigating it over the narrow lane in the heavy snow. He cursed to himself, low enough that his superior in the rear would not hear.

The chauffeur, a low-ranking KGB officer, had no idea why every morning for the past week they had driven from the warmth of Moscow into the forests of Valentinovka. There must be something big afoot. Perhaps at last they were planning to invade Western Europe?

"Itek . . ."

"Yes, sir?"

"Can you go no faster?"

"Faster, yes, Comrade General . . . faster."

For the next five minutes he pushed the big car up to a dangerous speed on the slick road. Then, when he was sure the general had fallen back into his own deep thoughts, he slowed back to a crawl.

It is I who will get shot, Comrade General, if I wrap this lumbering piece of shit around a tree!

The uniformed man in the rear of the Chaika was General Ivor Yuryevich Shalin, and the last thing on his mind was war or the weather, or the well-being of his chauffeur.

General Shalin was thinking about the many years it had taken to amass the power he now held, and what he must do to hold on to that power.

The car lurched to a halt in front of a massive wooden gate between two stone pillars. A uniformed sentry stepped from a tiny warming house and approached the car. He spoke hurriedly to the driver and leaned forward to shine a powerful light on Shalin in the rear seat.

Immediately, he snapped to attention and saluted.

Shalin returned the salute and the gates swung open.

Beyond the gate the lane turned into a wide avenue. It was bordered on each side by tall, majestic trees. At the end of the avenue, lights blazed in the sprawling, two-story dacha. It was dark green with lighter green trim and shutters, and nearly every window of its twenty rooms was bright.

How different was the opulence of this country house from the drab blocks of apartment buildings populated by the masses in Moscow.

But then it was bound to be more opulent. The dacha was the residence of the most powerful man in the Soviet Union: the former head of the KGB, and now the

Chairman of the Politburo, Yuri Vladimirovich Andropov.

The Chaika stopped between a Zil and a Volga KGB-licensed sedan. The door was immediately opened by a shivering soldier, and Shalin stepped out. The front door of the dacha was also opened for Shalin, and he stepped into a large center hall, the floor of which was dotted with priceless Oriental rugs, the wood of its walls polished to a sheen.

On the right was a lavishly furnished parlor illuminated by an enormous chandelier.

In the room were twenty or more men, some in uniform, most in civilian clothes—Savile Row suits tailored in London.

Shalin returned their nods and mounted a wide staircase with dark red carpeting and a wide, carved teak banister. At the top he opened one of two tall double doors and entered a brightly lit anteroom.

Two junior officers came to attention. A trio of doctors rose from high-backed chairs and quickly approached Shalin. He noticed that all three of them appeared shaken.

"Comrade General," said the taller of the three, "he is very angry. He has been asking for you all morning."

"The storm is getting heavier. It was hell getting out of Moscow."

"You are to go right in," growled another of the doctors.

One of the uniformed men opened the door. Shalin shucked his uniform greatcoat, passed it to the soldier, and entered.

It was an enormous room, with fifteen-foot-high ceilings, book-lined walls, and a large fireplace in which a huge log was burning. Placed at strategic intervals around an enormous bed were easy chairs, sofas, and several marble-topped tables.

A heavy-bodied nurse with a prunelike face stood as Shalin approached the bed. She leaned over the figure occupying it, spoke a few whispered words, and quickly departed.

When the door closed behind her, the figure spoke. "Comrade General Shalin."

He stepped forward as the white head managed to roll its sunken eyes in his direction. "Yes, Comrade Chairman."

"I have made my decision."

"Yes."

"I see no need to retain the files . . ." Shalin started to object, but an upraised, bony hand stopped him. "They have served their purpose. I have been an influence on the party and on my country because of them."

How well I know, thought Shalin. *Wasn't it I, starting out as a young KGB lieutenant, who did all the dirty work to amass them?*

"Power will shift without upheaval. I have made sure of everything."

You have made sure of nothing, Yuri Vladimirovich. Even now they are jockeying downstairs along with others in Moscow for the power you think you have passed on so easily.

"As for you, my old friend, I have taken pains to ensure your safety and your continued place in the scheme of things."

You only think you have, Yuri. Your corpse will barely be cold before the jackals will gather to devour me.

"Give me your key and the magnetic card, Ivor Yuryevich. I will have the box brought to us when the time comes and destroy the roll of microfilm. It is the best way . . . now."

"You are sure, Comrade Chairman?"

"Positive. Only now, near death, do I fully realize what harm that microfilm could reap. Too many heads would fall should all that information slip into hands unable to wield, with discretion, the power it carries."

The two men's eyes met and held. The inference was clear. The dying man was telling his old cohort—literally his partner in crime and potential blackmail—that he, Shalin, was the wrong man to hold such power.

Andropov had been, even in the days before becoming head of the world's largest and most powerful intelligence organization, an astute political strategist as well as a survivor.

As he gained power within the KGB, he forgot nothing and used everything. When he became head of the agency, he catered to those above him in power while, all the while, recording definitively their foibles and their mistakes.

These vast records held by a man with vast power proved their worth when Brezhnev gave up the ghost and the jockeying for real power began.

Shalin chewed his inner lip, trying to make his mind work, trying to conjure up excuses not to pass over his share of the power he had helped create.

"Comrade General . . ."

Keeping his face expressionless, the general withdrew a gold chain from beneath his tunic. From it he took a key, and placed it in the shaking hand.

"The card, Ivor Yuryevich."

From his wallet Shalin took a plain white card with magnetic wires embedded in its face and placed it over the key. The white head came up, the eyes blinked and focused on his hand, and then the fingers closed over key and card.

"Tired now, old friend, very tired. I must rest. I will call for you when my strength is better, and we will have the box brought to us."

"Of course, Comrade Chairman."

Shalin retreated two paces, bowed slightly, and left the room. The nurse immediately took his place, and Shalin motioned to the chief physician.

"Tell me, Comrade Doctor," Shalin asked in practically a whisper, "how long?"

"I am sorry, Comrade General, but I am not allowed—"

"Damn you for the pompous *zhopa* you are, man. The Chairman has given me a delicate piece of state business which must be timed perfectly. I must know!"

The chief physician bridled. He was the most respected physician in all Russia and the private doctor to the Chairman himself. He was not used to anyone calling him an ass.

But the gruff intensity in Shalin's voice warned him not to push his position. The eyes boring into him also warned him. Shalin's look was menacingly dangerous, ominous.

The doctor knew the man, Shalin, knew that he had come up through the ranks with the former KGB chief. He also knew that Shalin had carried out more than one assassination for his superior, and probably a great many more on his own.

"Well?" Shalin demanded.

"He has a few days . . . three at the most."

"You could be mistaken," Shalin replied. "He looks bad . . . as though it could happen within the hour."

The doctor shook his head. "Not likely. His vital signs are still fairly strong. It is a slow, insidious thing."

"You're sure . . . two or three days?"

A shrug. "As sure as I can be."

"Does he know?"

"Not really. I see no reason to predict the time of a man's death to his face."

There was a trace of a smile on Shalin's lips. "Good,

very good. Make sure that he rests comfortably."

Without waiting for a response, Shalin left the anteroom. But instead of turning right toward the front
staircase that would lead him down to the others, he
turned left. At the end of the hall he entered a study.
Without turning on a light, he moved to a bookcase and
felt until he found a hidden button.

A section of the bookcase swung silently open on
well-oiled hinges. Behind it was a steep flight of stairs.
An overhead light had come on automatically. At the
foot of the stairs was a solid steel door with a small slit
where the knob and keyhole would normally be.

Again Shalin fished in his wallet, and withdrew a
card. He gritted his teeth, swearing to himself that he
would personally strangle the young technician who had
duplicated the card if the copy didn't work.

It did.

The door rolled soundlessly open. Behind it were the
secret files and papers of the dying man upstairs.

Shalin knew just which box would be unlocked by the
duplicate key. He had accompanied his superior nearly
two months before, when they had both descended these
stairs and put the roll of microfilm to rest, supposedly
for the last time.

*Here is a second key and card, Ivor Yuryevich. We
have achieved our goals, but with these you will be my
insurance policy.*

And now, Shalin thought, turning the key and opening the drawer, *I* will have the insurance policy—and all
the power it holds—all to myself.

Inside the drawer was a black box. It took a combination of the card and the key to open the box.

Comrade General Shalin pocketed the roll of microfilm and locked everything back up.

Ten minutes later he was back in the Chaika, urging
his chauffeur to drive faster back to Moscow.

• • •

Andrei Charnovich was dreaming. It was definitely one of his better dreams. There was a girl in it who looked like his childhood sweetheart, only now she was all grown up and beautiful.

She was naked, on a bed, and she was motioning Andrei to join her. His feet were leaden; he couldn't make them move fast enough. When they began to move at last, the telephone ruined the dream.

Then he rolled over in the bed and his hand struck his wife's large, flabby rump.

That, and the shrill telephone, brought him wide awake. He reached across the mountain of his wife's body and spoke into the mouthpiece.

"Da?"

"Charnovich?"

"Da."

The caller spoke in a low, confidential tone. "This morning, Charnovich, we will again have need of your taxi service."

"A special fare?"

"Da."

"Where?"

The caller gave him the route, and Charnovich memorized it as the familiar voice spoke.

"How soon?"

"Her light is on now. I would imagine another thirty minutes."

"I will be there."

Charnovich yawned, replaced the phone, and swung his thin legs over the edge of the bed. As usual, he yelped when his feet hit the icy floor. As he stood to strip off his pajamas, his wife's muffled voice came from under the quilt.

"What is it?"

"A special fare."

"At this hour? You've only been home three hours!"

"Shut up, woman. I must work long and hard. How else could you afford to eat so much and live in a private apartment?"

Charnovich dressed and went out into the cold, snowy dawn, whistling to himself.

He let the Volga warm up a couple of minutes and then backed into the street. He paid no attention to the dark automobile parked inconspicuously at the curb a half block away. Nor did he pay any attention when the parked car pulled away from the curb without headlights and swung in behind him.

But he knew they were there. Later, they would be his witnesses.

Andrei Charnovich didn't get his fat salary, his private apartment, and many other perks for just driving his cab.

He got all those things by having accidents.

Angelina Galadin stepped from her apartment house and bent her head into the wind and snow. Even though it was a wide thoroughfare, Leninsky Prospekt was free of pedestrians and there was very little auto traffic. Part of this was because of the early hour in this section of the city. A second reason was the awful weather.

Every native in Moscow would be late to work this morning. And if Angelina Galadin were Russian, going to a Russian job from which she couldn't be fired, she, too, would probably be late.

But she wasn't, so she pulled the fur collar of her coat higher around her head and trudged onward.

She took a shortcut through a narrow alley, and turned left on Makarenko Ulica. It was a long four blocks to Zukovsk, where she would turn right.

The snow was deep, nearly to the top of her boots, making her thankful again that in a short time she would be in her beloved sunny, warm Spain.

She was nearly at the corner of Zukovsk, when she heard the roaring engine behind her. For a second she paid no attention.

Then, as it grew louder and seemed to be bearing directly at her, she turned.

She saw the two headlights heading straight for her.

She screamed.

And the last thing she saw before she was hurled, lifeless, through the air was the flickering TAXI sign in Cyrillic letters on the roof.

The Malagav on Gorki Street is famous all over Moscow for its spicy Georgian food. It is the favorite restaurant of high-ranking party members and the military who can afford it. Because of the status of its clientele, the Malagav also sports attentive, jovial waiters, as opposed to the usual sullen Moscow restaurant help.

General Ivor Shalin was recognized the moment he walked into the foyer. The headwaiter made the usual fuss, and at the general's command led him to a table already occupied by Gregor Leventov.

Leventov was a short, fat, balding man with a florid face dominated by a potatolike nose. Leventov was a KGB colonel, and worldwide liaison for the Soviet national airline, Aeroflot.

It was because of his position with Aeroflot that Shalin had long ago brought him into the scheme. No one would question Leventov's orders about what went on an airplane, or when. He himself also had unlimited —and unquestioned—travel abroad at any time.

"Good day, Ivor Yuryevich."

"Gregor," Shalin said with a nod, seating himself and carefully studying the other man.

Leventov's right hand, as he poured vodka for both of them, shook noticeably, as did his left using a handkerchief to mop the constant sweat from his face.

"How much of this have you had, Gregor?" Shalin asked once the headwaiter had left.

"A few glasses," the man admitted, and smiled lamely. "I am Russian."

"Today is February eighth, my dear Gregor. Let it be a day of triumph and not a day of drunkenness."

Shalin's tone was like ice. Leventov feared the KGB general, but on this day, in light of what they were doing, he feared his own fear much more. He set the glass of vodka down without drinking.

"Tell me!"

Shalin sipped. "Two . . . perhaps three days."

"Damn, we must move very quickly."

"We will," Shalin replied. "I have the film."

The man's eyes gleamed. "Where?"

"Here." Shalin leaned forward with his right arm under the table and dropped the small package in the other man's lap.

"Oh, my God."

"We don't believe in God, Gregor. Put it in your pocket and stop sweating."

Gregor Leventov couldn't stop sweating. Nor could he stop his hand from shaking as he slipped the fate of half the high-ranking leaders of the Soviet Union into his pocket.

Shalin had told him—only partially, he was sure—what the roll of microfilm contained. But even that much was enough to rock the very core of the Politburo for the next ten years.

"That is our future, Gregor . . . yours, Gusenko's, and mine. With the contents of that file we will have the power behind the thrones. Guard it carefully." Shalin paused, leaning forward. When he spoke again, it was in an even lower voice. "The Spanish woman?"

"Taken care of, a few hours ago. It was declared an

accident, even a possible suicide. The body is in the public morgue in Kalitnikovskaja."

"And the taxi driver?"

"The shock of the accident brought on a heart attack. He will be buried quietly."

"Good. Nikolai Gusenko has been informed?"

"I will accompany the body to Paris. Gusenko will take it from there to Madrid and turn it over to the family."

Shalin chuckled and lifted his glass. "And our little insurance policy will be in the vault. *Na zdorov'e*, Gregor. It is a new day."

In the kitchen, a waiter made a note in a small book that he had observed Comrade Gregor Leventov and Comrade General Shalin lunching together that day.

It was routine. Observation and filing boring reports were part of his second job . . . that of a watcher for the KGB.

The four aides were amazed. For as long as they had served the Chairman, spent time in the dacha, they had not known of the existence of the secret vault.

They took the black box and returned to the Chairman's bed, fearing yet another outburst of wrath. An hour before, his condition had taken a rapid turn for the worse. Yet, when it had happened, he had somehow summoned the strength for one last act.

Just minutes before, he had sent for General Shalin. When he was told that the general couldn't be found in the dacha and it was presumed that he had returned to Moscow, the room had erupted.

Shortly after that they had been given a card and a key and the instructions they were now carrying out.

"Comrade Chairman, the box you requested."

The dying man applied the card and key himself.

When he opened the lid his face regained much of its

former color, only to fade quickly to a sickly, greenish white.

He ordered everyone from the room except the highest-ranking members. To them he told the story.

And his last utterance before sinking back on the pillow was, "... Get it back ... and ... kill Shalin!"

TWO

Milan, February 1984

The taxi wound its way north from the Piazza del Duomo to the Piazza della Scala. At last the cab stopped near the alley running between La Scala itself and the building housing the museum next door.

"As far as I can go, signore. The stage door is down there."

"Grazie," Nick Carter replied, paid him with a liberal tip, and stepped from the cab.

Just before he moved down the alley, he glanced at the posters outside the theater. La Scala is of course famous for its opera the world over, and has been since the house was built in 1778 on the site of the Church of Santa Maria della Scala. But now posters proclaimed a three-night run of the Ballet de Paris, opening the following night.

The stage door read Artists Entrance. Not hesitating, Carter used his shoulder and managed to get inside.

"Signore?" He was about a hundred years old, and wore a black uniform with a matching billed cap that hid half his face.

"My name is Carter, Amalgamated Press and Wire Services. I have an appointment to interview Nina Cavetti."

Carter flashed his credentials. The guard bobbed his bill and ran a gnarled finger down a book of scrawled names. When he found the right one, he waved a finger toward a flight of steps.

"Dressing room Three, but they are probably on stage rehearsing."

"*Grazie,*" Carter said, but the old guard already had his newspaper back in front of his face and could care less.

The door marked "3" was open and empty. Carter moved on past more open dressing rooms to another flight of stairs that led down to the vast stage itself.

Everything was confusion. Short, fat women ran everywhere carrying costumes, while dancers in rehearsal clothes warmed up with bored expressions on their faces. One young man—or at least Carter thought it was a young man—jumped high in the air, made two complete revolutions, and came down on his crotch.

"Ouch," Carter groaned.

"*Pardon?*"

"Nothing."

The young man began stretching, the pain of his art evident on his face. Then he practiced his airborne pirouettes once again.

Carter moved on, scanning faces.

Stagehands, carrying scenery, shouted to one another

in Italian and at the dancers to get out of their way in French. Below, in the pit, an orchestra was tuning up, and sounded loud and awful. But Carter wasn't there to critique music or dance.

He was there answering a summons for help from a lovely Russian dancer that he had gotten out of a very tight spot in Budapest two years earlier. Her name was Nina Kovich then, and she had been defecting with her husband, a physics professor from Moscow State University.

The defection had backfired. They had been fingered, and in the attempted arrest Kovich had been killed.

The rules of the game concerning defectors—as laid down by Washington—could be summarized as follows: if they don't got something we particularly want, we don't want 'em.

Kovich's brain, and what was in it, Washington wanted. His wife's pliés and arabesques they didn't need.

But when the professor was shot, Carter couldn't exactly leave his wife stranded to take the heat.

He got her out, to Vienna and eventually to Paris. Once there, he pulled a few strings in the French bureaucracy and got her papers with a new identity. Nina Kovich became Nina Cavetti, complete with an Italian passport and a background from one of the best ballet schools in Rome.

She also got some money, a sympathetic shoulder to cry on from Carter, and a number to call with a code word if she ever needed some help.

Two days before, a call on that number had come through.

Carter always kept a promise.

Six feet of legs in tights bounced by and Carter stopped her. "Excuse me . . ."

"Oui?"

"Nina Cavetti?"

"Oui?"

"I'm a reporter. I'm supposed to interview her."

"Oui."

"I wonder if you could tell me where she is."

"Somewhere, here."

The dervish whirled off, and Carter moved on toward a group of dancers in tights, T-shirts, and leg warmers, which seemed to be the standard costume.

"I doubt that you are the new member of the corps de ballet."

The voice was female and it came from behind him. The French was pure but with an odd lilt.

Carter turned to find a very pretty young woman wearing black tights and a white T-shirt through which gleamed two small, compact breasts.

"No, I'm a little too old and beat up for this, I'm afraid," Carter replied with a grin.

She laughed. It was a nice laugh, even though the rubber band in her mouth did strange things to the sound. She had been running a brush through her long hair. Now she stopped, pulled it back, and fastened it with the rubber band.

Suddenly it hit him . . . the slight tilt of the head, the wry smile, the diminutive yet sensual figure . . .

"My God, Nina . . ."

The smile broadened. "Your Dr. Zeissdorf in Geneva was wonderful, no?"

Carter nodded dumbly.

Aaron Zeissdorf was a plastic surgeon. He specialized in rehabilitation, only now and then doing a purely cosmetic job.

In Nina's case he had done a complete makeover. When Carter had brought her out she had been rather plain, with a slight hook in her nose, a somewhat receding chin, and honey-blond hair.

Now she was a sable brunette with a pretty, pixieish face, not beautiful but definitely worth a second and a third look.

"I didn't know you went through with it," he said.

"I thought it best, a complete transformation." Here she paused to laugh. "Of course, being a very natural blonde, the hair poses a constant problem. It must be done every few days."

"And this?" Carter said, rolling his eyes around the vast stage.

"To be anonymous, I thought it best to be obvious. I think it has worked out quite well."

"Good." Carter relaxed and lit a cigarette. "Now, why the call?"

She glanced anxiously toward the other dancers milling around. The orchestra was still warming up. The principals hadn't arrived yet. The noise was rising to a deafening level.

"I think it best we not talk here. We only have one more number to rehearse. Could you wait? We could go somewhere out of the way for a drink or something."

Carter nodded. "Sure."

She slipped away and Carter moved out to the rear of the huge house. He had barely settled into a box when the dancers gathered on stage. After a few directions from a tall, big-boned man, the orchestra blared and the number began. Instantly, all that had been chaos suddenly became order and symmetry.

Carter, amazed at the transformation, tried to watch it with interest, but he'd always found classical ballet too artificial for his taste. Besides, his eyes kept wandering to the right where the man—Carter wondered if he was the dance master—stood.

He was about thirty and, for a dancer, rather tall and muscular, with black curly hair and stark blue eyes. Even from such a distance, Carter could see a thin scar that ran from behind his right ear, down his neck, and disappeared beneath his T-shirt.

There was something very familiar about the man, but no matter how hard the Killmaster concentrated, he couldn't place what it was.

Eventually the leaping and whirling figures on stage garnered his attention and the man slipped from his mind.

It took about a half hour to iron out the kinks to everyone's satisfaction before a halt was called. The company was admonished to relax until opening, and dismissed.

Carter returned backstage just as Nina was exiting, heading for her dressing room.

"How did you like it?"

"Wonderful," Carter replied.

"Liar. You didn't understand a bit of it," she teased.

"You're right. Change—I need a drink."

"I'll only be a minute."

She moved away to her dressing room and Carter got out of the crowd. He lounged in some shadows and studied the group, comparing them to a program he had picked up as he came down the aisle.

He wondered just how safe Nina was. At least a third of the performers had Russian names. Were they all defectors? And if they were, surely one of them would recognize Nina, if not by her face, at least by her style of dance.

Carter knew very little about ballet, but he had read enough to know that style and technique varied from country to country, and that Russian training was unique and highly valued by those in the dance world.

He glanced up to see the tall, blue-eyed man eyeing him from the edge of the stage. Up close he looked more like a longshoreman than a dancer. He had shoulders like a boxer, and heavy arms. Then Carter glanced at his hands, and little bells went off.

The joints of his fingers were oversize, as if they were swollen, and there were calluses on the sides of the palms.

They were not the hands of a dancer, Carter knew. Carter's own mangled hands had the same appearance, and it was caused by daily training, pounding his fists against anything that would harden them. The knuckles were oversize because they had been broken and allowed to mend slightly out of joint. Because of this, hardened scar tissue made them stronger and impervious to pain when they struck something . . . like an artery in the neck, crushing it.

They were the hands of a killer.

Then Nina appeared beside Carter. She looked lost in a dark cotton dress, heavy leggings that came to her knees, and an oversize fur coat.

Once a Russian, Carter thought, always a Russian.

"Shall we go?"

"Sure," he said, taking her arm. "Don't turn around, but the guy who gave all the directions on stage . . . is he the dance master?"

"No, he's the first assistant stage manager. We have a lazy dance master who gives him orders and he relays them."

"I didn't think he looked like a dancer."

Nina laughed. "He isn't. But he seems to be a good technician. I suppose that was why he was hired."

Carter checked the program. "Duval?"

She nodded. "Henri Duval."

Carter asked her about the preponderance of Russian names in the program as they hit the street. It brought another, louder laugh to her lips.

"Stage names. Everyone believes that the only real training in ballet comes from Russia. So, no matter who anyone is, they take a Russian stage name when they look for work."

She took the program from his hand and ran a finger

down the list before raising it to his eyes.

"This one, Boris Charkovsky?"

"Yeah."

"His real name is François Lessing. A Paris agent found him dancing nude in a Marseille bordello. But, believe it or not, he's a very well-trained dancer."

Carter shook his head. "The vagaries of show business."

The rental car was a small Mercedes. Carter handed Nina in, and went around to the driver's side. He didn't speak until they were headed north on the wide Via Brera.

"Want to tell me now?" he asked at last.

She tucked her legs beneath her and turned partially toward him in the passenger seat. Out of the corner of his eye Carter could see her face become serious.

"I don't think I ever told you, but I still have family in the Soviet Union."

"No, you didn't."

"I do, a brother. He tried to join my husband and me when we came out, but he couldn't get a travel permit to Budapest. He's been trying to get out ever since."

Carter lit a cigarette and inhaled deeply before replying. "And now he's coming out?"

"Yes."

"When?"

"Tomorrow night, through Finland. At least, that is the plan."

"Does he have help?"

Carter maneuvered the car through a sudden burst of traffic. When they were clear again she still hadn't answered. He glanced over to see her puffing nervously on a cigarette, inhaling deeply and almost gasping out the smoke.

"I didn't know dancers smoked."

"They are the worst smokers," Nina replied, crushing out the butt and immediately lighting another.

"You haven't answered my question."

"I know. Yes, he has help . . . from the KGB."

"What?"

She waved the cigarette in the air. "He's doing some special job for them. In return, they are giving him travel papers. When he gets to Helsinki he will just defect."

Carter frowned in concentration. "It sounds a little too pat for me. What kind of a job is he doing?"

"I don't know. Even he didn't know until a day or so ago, and I haven't been in contact with him since."

"Nina, *any* kind of job your brother would do for the KGB is going to be shady as hell. And if it's shady enough, they won't want him walking around talking about it, especially in the West."

"I know. Joseph felt the same way. That's why he has taken some precautions."

"What kind of precautions?"

"The KGB is giving him travel papers from Moscow to the frontier of Finland. He will go by train to Helsinki. But if they try to stop him—or worse—he has an alternate route."

She laid out both sides of the plan, and Carter listened closely as he drove.

Then he spotted the restaurant he wanted, and conversation ceased as he parked.

"Quaint," Nina commented, staring at the building.

"And out of the way," Carter replied, guiding her to the door.

The restaurant was called Bella Marlene. It stood alone on a street of aging tenements and looked like a miniature Venetian palazzo. With its chipped stonework and weathered paint, it had an unkempt look, like the neighborhood. It had diamond-patterned stained-glass windows and an old-fashioned post lantern by the door that cast a weak yellow light.

"You've been here before?" Nina asked.

"Often. The owner is a friend, a Welshman named Scudder."

"A Welshman? In Milan?"

Carter chuckled. "He has the soul of an Italian."

Inside was sedate opulence, with crystal chandeliers and private, curtained booths. Carter requested one of these and inquired about Scudder.

"He is in a meeting. It will last . . . perhaps an hour," replied the maître d'. "Could I give him your name, signore?"

"Carter. He'll know."

The Killmaster ordered for both of them a Lombardy stew of pork, sausages, carrots, and white wine, and a small side dish of polenta.

"I never knew your Italian was as fluent as your French," Nina said.

"So's my Russian," Carter said and grinned. "Let's speak English."

They waited until the food had arrived and they were halfway through the meal before they returned to the matter of Nina's brother.

"My family name was Kadinskov."

Carter nodded. "So what can I do for you and Joseph Kadinskov?"

"The same thing you did for me."

"Papers?" Carter said with a wry face.

She nodded. "New papers, for both of us."

"You're leaving the ballet?"

"Yes. I have put aside some money. I have made some contacts here in Italy. We can start a new life."

"You think that's wise?" Carter asked.

"I think it is necessary. Alone, I was able to hide. Together . . . it would be difficult. Can you help? I know it is asking a great deal. My brother has nothing your State Department wants, so help from that area is out. But you know so many people . . ."

Her words trailed off in a plea. Carter pushed his plate away and refilled their glasses.

"I do have a few people in the Italian CID that owe me a favor or two. We'll have to create a whole new background for both of you."

"I understand."

"And you want to stay in Italy?"

"Yes."

Carter paused, studying her, and then smiled. "I like your new look."

Nina returned the smile, moving her hands across the table to cover his. "Thank you, Nick. Thank you so very much."

"I'll have to list an occupation on the papers."

She thought for a moment. "Journalist. That would be far enough afield."

"Good enough. What does Joseph do now?"

She paused. "You'll laugh . . ."

"Try me."

"He's a mortician."

THREE

Joseph Kadinskov kept his shaggy blond head turned away from the body as he closed the valve and removed the needles from the corpse.

Odd, he thought. In his career he had embalmed over five hundred deceased, and not once had he ever had a shaking hand or a queasy feeling.

This night he had had both.

Absently, he pulled a rubber sheet up over the naked body to hide the grotesqueness of the empty stomach cavity held open by clamps.

He stopped the sheet at her chin and found that he couldn't cover her face. It was a beautiful face, even in death, and young.

"Animals," Kadinskov murmured aloud, "pure beasts."

He was about to step away from the steel-topped

table, when the medallion around her neck slipped, making a resounding clanking sound on the metal surface.

Suddenly the air in the concrete-lined cold room was more dank and chill than usual.

Catholic, Kadinskov thought, reaching for the medallion, *and no priest to give her last rites*.

The medallion, like the body and room, was cold in his fingers. On one side of it was an image of the Virgin, kneeling, her arms upraised to heaven. On the other side was an inscription in Spanish.

Kadinskov knew no Spanish, but he mouthed the words phonetically. Somehow they seemed to burn into his brain before he slipped the medallion back beneath the rubber sheet.

A single bell chimed, and he glanced up at the metal box near the ceiling. One single bulb of four glowed red, the rear entrance.

They had arrived.

He stripped off his rubber gloves and moved up the concrete stairs to the main floor. At the end of a long hall he opened a heavy steel door.

Three men stood just ouside the door in the alley. The short, fat one Kadinskov recognized as Gregor Leventov, even though the man had never offered his name in their previous talks. The two men who flanked Leventov wore broad-brimmed, dark hats and bulky coats. Their wide faces were devoid of expression and their eyes were dead. They were clones of a hundred others who passed in and out of KGB headquarters at 2 Dzerzhinsky Square daily.

Beyond the three men, Kadinskov could see a Zil limousine, a hearse, and a small Volga sedan parked in the alley.

Leventov didn't speak until the steel door was closed and secured behind them.

"We are alone here?" he asked.

"Of course. Everything is just as you stipulated, comrade. No one has seen the woman except myself."

"Where is she?"

"This way," Kadinskov replied, surprised at the calmness in his voice, "in the cold room."

They moved down the steps single file and entered the room. The two clones stayed in the background as Kadinskov and Leventov moved to the table. Without preamble, the KGB colonel ripped the sheet from the body.

Kadinskov winced but stayed silent.

"Good, Joseph Ivanovich, you have done well. Tell me, after she has been sewn up, will the scar seem only the result of an autopsy?"

"It should," Kadinskov replied. "Did you know she was pregnant?"

To Kadinskov's surprise, Leventov smiled broadly. He almost beamed at the news.

"No? Really? Excellent! It will make suicide a more acceptable reality to her death. You will put that in the report, of course."

Now Kadinskov did feel sick. He pulled on a fresh set of rubber gloves, and then kept his hands busy with instruments on a side table so they would be out of the other man's sight.

Out of the corner of his eye he saw Leventov withdraw a small, oilskin-wrapped package from his pocket.

"Proceed. Here is the package."

"My papers," Kadinskov replied.

"What?" The man's bushy gray eyebrows went up and his voice boomed in the small room.

"My papers . . . I want to see them, hold them."

Leventov exchanged looks with one of the other two men, and then returned his gaze to the mortician with a shake of his head.

"You worry me, Joseph Ivanovich. Do I sense mistrust in your voice?"

"No, comrade, I am simply, shall we say, a careful man. My papers?"

Using his free hand, Leventov withdrew an envelope from his coat pocket and passed it over.

Quickly, Kadinskov examined the contents. He sighed with relief. No matter how they tried to trick him now, at least he had a fighting chance to escape.

It was all there: an explicit route, travel papers inside the country, an exit visa, his passport, and a credit voucher for twenty thousand American dollars drawn on the Eurobank in Geneva, Switzerland.

"Satisfied, Joseph Ivanovich?"

"Very much so. Do you care to watch?"

"Very much so."

Kadinskov took the package. Carefully, he placed it in the stomach cavity. Then, just as carefully, he added a puttylike plastic substance from a tube to encase it and give the stomach fullness when it was closed.

This done, he removed the clamps and folded the skin flaps back together. Using his finest, most intricate stitch, he sutured the wound until it was tightly closed. At last he lifted his hands in a gesture of finality. "Done."

Leventov leaned close to the wound. He poked and probed until he seemed satisfied. "Is there any chance at all that the wound will be opened at the other end?"

Kadinskov shrugged. "There is always the chance if there is some question about the manner of death. It also depends on where the other end is."

Leventov seemed perplexed. He frowned, and at last seemed to shrug to himself, as if answering the man's question made no difference.

"Spain. She will be going to Madrid."

Kadinskov's stomach turned. The other man's ready

answer had told him worlds.

"I think she will be buried just as she is, comrade. And because her death is listed as a suicide, not in a Catholic cemetery. The Spanish revere death and have a great deal of respect for the remains. I doubt that anyone will check the body."

"Good. What else?"

"Just dress her. I retained the clothes she was wearing, there on that other table."

Leventov snapped his fingers. The two clones went into action. Kadinskov was drawn to the side.

"There are the certificates of release for the body, the embalming code and certificate, and your report on the state of the remains. Sign, Joseph Ivanovich, and pencil a notation on the bottom as to the pregnancy."

Kadinskov did as he was told, and then glanced quickly over the papers. "There is no name, comrade."

"That will be taken care of," Leventov said, snatching the papers. "Make yourself ready to leave."

"I'll get my bag."

Kadinskov moved from the cold room into his tiny office with a tight smile on his face.

So, he thought, Leventov had to tell him a few things, but not everything.

But it had been enough to warn him.

From a side pocket in his bag he took a Tokarev 7.62 automatic pistol. It was already loaded with eight rounds and equipped with a three-inch Czech-made silencer. He lowered his pants and slipped the automatic into a sling already wound around his right leg. He was just rebuckling his belt when Leventov called out to him.

"Coming, comrade, coming."

He jammed a fur hat on his head and pushed his arms into the cheap but warm and bulky cloth coat.

The two clones were carrying the body up the stairs

when he returned to the cold room. Leventov spoke as they climbed the steps.

"The driver will take you to Byelorussia Station. The Leningrad train leaves at precisely midnight. You will change to the train for Helsinki at Vyborg. From there, good luck to you, Joseph Ivanovich."

"Thank you, comrade."

"And, Kadinskov, I don't think I need remind you to talk to no one at the station here, at Vyborg, or at the frontier. Understand?"

"Of course."

Leventov left him at the car, strutted to the waiting Zil, and climbed into the back. Kadinskov settled into the rear seat of the Volga, and it lurched from the alley.

He moved into the opposite corner from the driver and slid his hand through the coat's slitted pocket. Gently he closed his fingers over the reassuring hardness of the Tokarev.

As he studied the back of the driver's head, he wondered where they would try to kill him.

General Ivor Shalin poked the button on the panel and the elevator swiftly lifted him through the center of the opulent apartment complex to the eighteenth floor.

His plans had been made for months, and clarified in the last twenty-four hours.

He had dismissed his driver for the night, but he retained a second set of keys to the Zil. His office had already been informed that he might be called away on a moment's notice for an inspection trip to Tallinn, in Estonia. If anything went wrong in the next day or two before the old man died, a fast boat would get him to safety in Helsinki.

He opened the door to his apartment, and even before he switched on the light he sensed their presence. Calmly, he flicked it on and smiled.

But the smile faded quickly. His beautiful apartment

was a shambles. Wallpaper and paneling had been ripped from the walls. The furniture had been shredded and his paintings ripped from their frames. Even the double French doors leading to the balcony had been taken from their hinges and ripped apart. Cold wind and snow gusted into the apartment.

The doors to both bedrooms were open, and he could see that they hadn't fared much better.

There were four of them, three men in civilian clothes and a woman in uniform with major's pips on her shoulder boards. Two of them he knew—the woman, and the small dark man on the sofa, whose hand rested possessively and protectively on a large black bag at his side.

"What is the meaning of this?" Shalin blustered. "I will have you all counting trees for this insult!"

The reference to being sent to Siberia caused no reaction. The four faces looking at him could have been carved from stone.

The woman stepped forward. She was tall, big-boned, and even in the somewhat ill-fitting uniform her figure was voluptuous. Her blond hair was pulled back into a tight bun and fastened beneath her garrison cap.

Relaxed, Shalin knew her as a beautiful woman, her features perfectly formed around large, ice-green eyes, her pale skin as smooth as stretched silk.

But now, standing with her hands folded beneath her breasts, her feet wide in a defiant stance, and her lips pressed tightly together, she looked like a viper about to strike.

"Comrade General, I am Major Anya Annamovna Chevola."

"I know who you are. What I want to know is on what authority have you done all this!"

"The highest authority, Comrade General, the very highest. And I think you know why we are here."

Shalin's eyes floated toward the dark little man sitting

so serenely on the sofa with the bag. His name was Anton Dubchov, and he held the distinction of being the
master interrogator of Lubyanka. Shalin had no doubt
that the bag he fondled so lovingly held the horrible
tools of his trade: tools Shalin had seen him use on
others many times in the secret bowels of the old prison.

Involuntarily, he shuddered.

"What do you want?" he demanded, forcing steel
into his voice.

"I think you already know the answer to that question as well, Comrade General. My orders come directly
from the Presidium of the Supreme Soviet. Obviously,
for security reasons, we cannot take you to Lubyanka.
That is the reason for Comrade Dubchov's presence."

"I see. Then I am not under arrest."

"Not officially."

"May I smoke?"

"No!" Her voice was an angry whiplash. "You are to
be interrogated, Ivor Yuryevich Shalin, for the crime of
theft against the state and treason against the party and
Soviet people."

Shalin kept up his bluff. "What is it I am supposed to
have stolen?"

"We do not have time to play the cat to your mouse,
comrade. Obviously, we have not found what we are
looking for in the apartment. Your briefcase."

Shalin handed it over. Both of the men searched it
thoroughly, and shook their heads toward the major.

"Comrade Shalin," she barked, "remove your
clothes!"

There is a feeling of utter defenselessness about complete nudity. Although one knows consciously that or-
dinary clothing gives no protection against lethal
weapons or modern forms of torture, there is an
unreasoning and panicky sense of vulnerability that ac-
companies nakedness.

The thought of it contracted Shalin's hard belly muscles and brought a faint mist of red over his eyes. He controlled himself with an effort as he walked across the room toward the liquor cabinet.

"What are you doing?" the woman hissed. "I have ordered you to remove your clothes!"

"I am going to have a drink, comrade," Shalin said, pouring himself a glass of vodka and retaining the bottle in his right hand.

Major Anya Chevola pulled a revolver from the holster at her waist. "You will do as I say, comrade, or they will do it for you."

"Come, come, Anya, do you take me for a fool? You won't shoot me without interrogating me first. And before I allow you to do that, I insist . . . no, I *demand* that you call Valentinovka. I want to talk to the Chairman."

Major Anya Chevola's lips turned downward in the most grotesque imitation of a smile Shalin had ever seen.

"I am afraid that is impossible. Comrade Chairman Andropov died two hours ago."

Shalin could not stop the color from draining out of his face. He could feel it and knew that the others saw it.

Just below and to his left, he heard a dull thud. He looked. Anton Dubchov was grinning up at him like a vulture. He had dropped the case open to display his instruments.

It was over. If he could talk to Andropov, appeal to their friendship, explain that he had only taken the microfilm for safekeeping until the time came to destroy it . . .

But he couldn't, not now. The empty box must have been discovered just before Andropov died, and the order given.

Dubchov began to unload his case.

No, Shalin thought, *never! I am a hero of the Soviet Union! I have followed the party line my whole life, degraded myself a thousand times over for the glory of another man!*

I will not be degraded again.

Suddenly, all Shalin's concentration was on Anton Dubchov's ugly, leering face.

He flipped the vodka bottle in his hand and caught it by the base. He whirled it so the hundred-proof vodka spurted out and into Dubchov's face and eyes.

The woman and one of the other men were stunned into immobility. The other man started toward Shalin.

Shalin continued the downward swing as Dubchov sputtered and dug his fingers into his blinded eyes. The neck of the bottle slammed against an edge of the cabinet and cracked off, so the jagged remains stayed in Shalin's hand.

The KGB man came after him with a long, arcing swing. The fist caught Shalin on the side of the head, momentarily staggering him. He avoided a second blow, sidestepped the man's body, and lurched around him.

He lunged forward with the saw-toothed weapon outthrust, ramming the jagged edges viciously into Anton Dubchov's throat, and twisted as he rammed.

There was one faint, inarticulate gurgle as Dubchov died horribly with the flesh of his face and throat in shreds and crimson blood gushing from the pierced jugular vein.

Shalin stood over him, breathing heavily, with the bottle still gripped in his hand and Dubchov's blood dripping from it down onto the faceless thing on the floor.

"Drop it, Comrade General! I will kill you if I must!" Anya Chevola shouted.

Her words slowly pierced the mist that had clouded Shalin's brain. He looked up to see the woman's steady hands aiming her revolver, her knuckles already white on the trigger. The two KGB agents were circling him. It would be only a matter of time before they could overpower him.

And then they would call for another Dubchov.

It was useless.

"I will kill you if I have to, comrade."

"I am well aware of that, Major," Shalin said, letting the bottle slip from his grasp to the floor.

The two men relaxed.

In that instant, Shalin turned and stepped out onto the balcony. He didn't stop. He just kept walking, right over the railing, bending at the waist and then plunging outward . . .

And down . . .

Eighteen stories.

The old Khodinsk field at the Moscow airport was rarely used. Now and then, soldiers rehearsing drill and parades for Red Square celebrations would fill its vastness with the thump of boots and martial music.

But on this night it was quiet except for the warming engines of a big Ilyushin transport. The plane was used mainly for foreign trade. Tonight it was flying to Paris with a load of textile dyes, flax, and fine finished lumber for furniture manufacture.

Rarely did these transport planes carry passengers. But this one had two: one dead, one alive.

The hearse proceeded through the heavily guarded gate without being stopped, as did the Zil limousine directly behind it. The two vehicles glided to a stop beside the huge gaping wound of the Ilyushin's loading bay.

Instantly, men scurried about transferring the casket. Gregor Leventov, carrying only a small overnight bag and the travel papers for his "cargo," stepped from the limousine and walked toward the load master, a GRU colonel.

"Good evening, comrade."

Leventov grunted a greeting and presented the papers. The colonel perused them quickly and glanced up as the tail end of the coffin disappeared into the hold of the Ilyushin.

"Chemicals, comrade?"

"Isn't that what it says, comrade?" Leventov said through gritted teeth.

The colonel glanced again at the papers, this time at the bottom. The signature of authorization was General Ivor Shalin.

"Of course, comrade. Use the forward boarding ladder, please."

Leventov hurriedly boarded the plane and settled into the small, six-seat passenger section directly behind the cockpit.

His timing had been perfect. He had barely buckled his safety belt when he heard and felt the shudder of the giant loading bay doors close. Seconds later the big plane nosed around and began to taxi.

Not until they were in the air did Leventov relax and take out a small flask of vodka.

In a few hours, his part of it would be over. In Paris he would hand the body over to Gusenko. Then, like Shalin, he would simply disappear for a week.

Hopefully, by that time, the Comrade Chairman would have departed for his last reward and the three of them—he, Shalin, and Gusenko—would resurface and inform the Politburo of the power they held.

He smiled.

The future for Gregor Leventov looked very rosy. Very rosy indeed.

FOUR

Carter sat back in the taxi, absorbing the jolts as the driver swerved and bumped over the uneven, potholed back road that took them from the country into the city of Helsinki.

It had been a rough eighteen or so hours, made up of a lot of hurried phone calls and one hell of a lot of traveling.

Luigi Corelli of Italian CID had long owed Carter a big one. He was more than willing to pay off, especially after Carter told him the circumstances. Background credentials and new identity papers would be no problem. The only hitch was, if Carter wanted them authentic, it would take at least a week.

That was too long, but it couldn't be helped.

The Killmaster bypassed this problem by making a

phone call to another old friend, Gustav Bijornan, in
Helsinki.

Yes, a couple of Finnish passports could be made
up in such a short time, particularly for the fee Carter
was suggesting. Of course, fine work would take much
longer, but if Carter could accept crude forgeries, Bijornan could accommodate him.

Crude forgeries would do to get them from Helsinki
to Rome. Once there, the forgeries would be destroyed
and the couple could get their authentic Italian papers.

From Milan to Helsinki, Carter had chosen the most
roundabout route possible. They had used cars, trains,
airplanes, and, once, for a short hop, an excursion boat.

Nina had told him such precautions weren't necessary. She was positive that her cover, particularly with
the plastic surgery, hadn't been breached.

Carter was taking no chances. There had been too
many times in the past when he had underestimated the
oblique deviousness of the KGB and their military
counterpart, the GRU. Each time he had, the mission
had been a failure.

This particular mission, helping Nina, wasn't official.
Actually, Carter had taken two weeks of his vacation to
respond to her call. But, to him, that didn't make it less
important.

They had arrived in Helsinki six hours before. Carter
had parked Nina in a hotel in the center of the city, and
met Bijornan. The forged documents would be ready
that evening. Did Carter have the photos?

The Killmaster passed them over and returned to the
hotel. They left without checking out, and, changing
cabs twice, drove far out of the city to a set of rustic
cabins on a large lake. There they registered as a honey-
moon couple with a mutual love of ice fishing.

The reason for this was twofold. The first, of course,
was to avoid detection if there had been an attempt

made to follow them. The second, the meet with Joseph Kadinskov once he was safely in Finland.

Kadinskov had already arranged with his sister that, if he were betrayed, he would leave the train before it reached the Helsinki station and make his way cross country to the village of Raija. From there he would trek southward to Lake Borga. If this was necessary, the meet would be twenty-four hours later than the original time at the central station in Helsinki.

The taxi nose-dived to a stop in the block between the central train station and the parliament building. Carter paid the driver and worked his way down the street, pausing now and then to gaze into shop windows.

He had taken every conceivable precaution, but something nagged him. He felt that he was being tailed, even though he could detect no one.

Finally he called it paranoia, and headed directly to the station. Just inside the vast main room, he paused.

She was there, reading, bundled up in her fur coat, sitting on a bench near the stairway up from the main tracks: Nina.

Again, to split up a tail or confuse one, Carter had told her to take a second cab into the city. This also made it easier for him to stay in the background and cover them both if Kadinskov arrived as scheduled.

Nina glanced up, caught Carter's eye for a second, and went back to her magazine.

He continued on through the huge rotunda and exited through a side door. Two blocks down Kaisanlemen Katu, he turned into an office building and took the elevator to the fifth floor. There he stepped out and walked up two more flights.

Gustav Bijornan's office was not much more than a cubbyhole at the end of a dim but spotlessly clean corridor. The sign on the door identified him as a dealer in fine gems.

It made Carter grin. Fine gems, yes, but more often than not, other people's.

He rang the buzzer sharply, waited a moment, and then tapped lightly, twice, on the paneling. Finally he heard the door's interior peephole cover slide away.

The voice from the other side was muffled and raspy. "That you, Nick?"

"Yes, Gustav—sorry I'm late."

"One moment."

Carter heard chains rattling and locks turning. The door opened wide and a bald head fringed with gray fuzz appeared in the crack. Two eyes, made enormous by half-inch-thick lenses, read Carter and the door was opened.

Carter stepped inside and Bijornan went through the locking ritual. At last he turned to face the Killmaster.

"The burdens of security," he said with a shrug.

Carter laughed. "How can that be, Gustav? You're the only criminal in Finland."

"True," the other man chuckled, "but we do get a youthful tourist now and then from Germany or America foolish enough to try and get his return passage by petty theft. Sit down."

The two men moved to chairs by a cluttered desk. Bijornan took two Finnish passports from a drawer and passed them over.

"Good. They look real."

"The shells are real," Bijornan said. "The signatures and the stamp, of course, are false. But they will do nicely to get your people out of the country."

Carter pocketed the passports and passed a thick envelope across the desk. A fat hand slid the envelope into a drawer.

"You're not going to count it?"

"My friend, you and I are honest men," Bijornan said with a smile and a shrug. "But let me caution you.

Of all the frontiers in the world, those will be spotted by the Soviets or any of their satellites.''

Carter chuckled. ''Not to worry, Gustav. They are coming out, not going in.''

''I thought as much, but still . . .''

The old man stood. Carter shook his hand and left. On the street he checked his watch. It was ten minutes until the arrival of the Moscow-Vyborg train.

He set off for the central station.

On the Moscow-to-Vyborg leg, Joseph Kadinskov shared a compartment with a woman, her small son, and a Finnish businessman who spoke Russian with a terrible accent. Kadinskov quickly decided that none of them posed a threat.

Changing cars in Vyborg, he spent most of the time in the men's toilet, emerging and boarding only minutes before his train number was called.

The new coach was practically empty, and Kadinskov had the compartment to himself.

An hour later they reached the frontier. Outside, it had stopped snowing, but gazing across the vast open whiteness he could sense the bitter cold that would await him if he had to leave the train and strike off across the countryside on foot.

He hoped that wouldn't be necessary, but deep down in his heart of hearts he was sure they were not going to let him go.

Customs and border patrol guards worked their way down the car, rudely interrogating each person as they examined their papers. At last they reached Kadinskov.

''Your papers, comrade.''

The customs official—who was also a low-ranking officer in the KGB—was a small, swarthy man with darting, birdlike eyes and a beaked nose. He was dwarfed by the two uniformed guards behind him.

If his eyes could ignite, Kadinskov thought, the passport and travel papers in his hands would be in flames.

"Why do you leave the motherland, comrade?"

"Business, in Helsinki."

"And how long do you plan on staying?"

"Just two days."

"Your papers are not in order."

"What?" Kadinskov couldn't keep the color in his face as he jumped to his feet. "What do you mean?"

"Your interior travel permit is only one-way, Moscow to the frontier."

Kadinskov inspected the paper and felt his knees go weak. "It must be just an oversight, in Moscow."

"Perhaps . . ."

The ugly little man seemed to be staring right into his brain. This was a wrinkle Kadinskov hadn't dreamed would occur. It probably had been an oversight on Leventov's part. He was going just one way.

Damn the bureaucratic mind, he thought. Would he be taken from the train because of this foolishness?

"You will have to apply at the frontier on your return for a travel permit to Moscow, comrade."

"Yes, yes, of course, I'll do that."

The little man handed over his papers and moved on down the coach. Kadinskov sagged back in the seat with an audible sigh.

But relief didn't completely envelop him until the train started moving again.

And then they were over, across the frontier, into Finland. Even the snow outside the window, glistening in the winter sun, seemed cleaner.

It was 161 kilometers from the frontier to Helsinki central station, with three stops in between. Because of heavy snow and delays for traffic having the right of way in the other direction, it was almost two hours before the train stopped again.

Kadinskov rubbed the condensation from the glass and stared out at the platform. Two passengers got off. He counted five waiting to board, and mentally catalogued them.

Two pretty teen-age girls. An ancient woman in a coat much too thin for the weather carrying two cloth-wrapped bundles. A well-dressed older man nervously smoking a cigar. A stooped old man in a black greatcoat with a red-tipped white cane and dark glasses.

The cigar smoker, Kadinskov thought, perhaps.

He arranged himself on the seat, slid his hand through the slit in the coat pocket, then under his belt. He eased the Tokarev from its sling and slitted his eyes, feigning sleep.

The train lurched forward. He waited, and waited. Minutes passed and no one came.

Surely they would have all dispersed through the train by now, he thought.

He was about to end the charade and sit up, when the compartment door opened and the blind man tapped his way to the seat across from Kadinskov.

He knew. He didn't know how he knew, but he just did.

Of course. It made good sense. Why do it inside the Soviet Union where questions could be raised, because his body would surely be identified eventually? But here, in Finland, if the body were stripped of all identification and the cause of death appeared to be a heart attack . . .

An investigation would go only so far and then be dropped.

The cane. Kadinskov studied it, the narrowing of the shaft to the tip.

In his line of work he had seen and worked on many victims. Always he was instructed to leave from his report any mention of the tiny puncture wound in the shoulder, thigh, or buttocks.

He strained to stay relaxed and maintain the posture of sleep as he went over in his mind the five most toxic elements in the world.

There were diptheria and tetanus germs, as well as botulinus, twice as strong as cobra venom. Merely one gram could kill 36,000 people. There was rien, a deadly derivative of the castor oil plant.

But all four of those took time, as long as ten days.

But, with the right dosage, gramicidin was instant. In small amounts it could be used for punishment or torture. In larger amounts it turned a man into a vegetable in seconds, mobile but incoherent. Death usually occurred within an hour, more than enough time to send him tumbling from the train onto the frozen tundra.

Through slitted eyes, Kadinskov looked at the dark glasses. He sensed that the eyes behind those glasses were not sightless. They were watching him, weighing him.

He saw the cane lift, and tightened his grip on the Tokarev. The center of the cane rested on the man's knee, the hand holding it curled, preparing to thrust.

When it did, Kadinskov kicked it aside with his foot and fired. Nervous reaction made him fire three times when once would have been sufficient.

All three slugs entered the left side of the man's chest, killing him instantly.

Smoke and a small spurt of flame erupted from the hole in Kadinskov's coat. Quickly he pulled his left hand up into his sleeve and beat it out.

Then he examined the man he had just killed. Death had been immediate, with little or no blood.

He removed the dark glasses and shoved them into his own pocket. As he suspected, the passport and other papers were Finnish. Kadinskov couldn't tell, but he guessed they were phony. These, too, he placed in his own pocket. When he could find no other papers or identification on the body, he checked the corridor.

Empty.

He took a flask of vodka from his bag and held it, untapped, in his left hand and hoisted the man with his right arm.

He was almost to the end of the corridor when the well-dressed businessman emerged from a compartment.

Kadinskov drank lustily from the flask and greeted the man in a slurred voice. At the same time, he shielded the front of the body from view.

The cigar smoker made a wry face and squeezed by them.

Kadinskov carried his burden to the platform between cars. He propped the body up in a corner and lit two cigarettes. One he smoked himself, the other he stuck between the dead man's lips.

Then he opened the top half of the door and waited, every few minutes leaning out to look down the tracks.

Two passengers walked through, neither of them paying any attention to the two lolling drunks.

Kadinskov looked out again. Five hundred yards ahead was a tunnel.

He readied the body, and the moment they were engulfed in darkness, he heaved it through the opening. He closed the upper half of the door, and by the time the train emerged from the tunnel, he was back in his compartment.

A half hour later the train stopped in the tiny village of Isvit. Kadinskov got off and went directly to the men's room. He changed into heavy outdoor clothes and snow boots. The bag he shoved to the bottom of a large waste can.

For the next half hour he wandered the streets of the

small village until he found a small garage that rented snowmobiles.

The young man was most obliging, even telling Kadinskov the best places within a five-mile radius for ice fishing.

It was ironic.

He rented the snowmobile with the dead man's credentials, and paid for it with the Finnish markkas he had taken from the body.

Carter paid the cabdriver at the road and walked up the long, snow-covered lane to the cabin. He could see by the fresh tracks that Nina had already arrived.

In his mind he could still see the stark look of fear on her face when the last of the train's passengers had passed through the exit turnstiles and her brother had not been among them.

It was all on her face—another eighteen hours of agony until the alternate meet. And perhaps there would be no second meeting. Joseph might not have gotten out at all.

She was sitting, still in her huge coat, her head in her hands, when Carter came in. Beside her, the fire they had banked before leaving still smoldered. She didn't look up.

Carter set the bag of groceries he had purchased before leaving Helsinki on a table, and silently stoked the fire. When it was blazing and its heat had permeated the small room, he took a bottle of Finnish vodka from the bag, found two glasses, and joined her.

"Here—there's nothing we can do now until tomorrow."

Nina took it and drank. Her eyes were red-rimmed. Carter couldn't help wondering what she would do if her brother didn't make it. She had walked out on the ballet world, literally disappeared, so that avenue was

no longer open to her. That would also, more than
likely, kill the Cavetti alias she had been using.

Suddenly Carter didn't want to think about it.

"Hungry?"

She shrugged.

"We're both hungry," he said, and unpacked the
food he had bought.

He managed a poor imitation of a smörgasbörd, and
laid out slices of thick-crusted Finnish bread heavy with
sweet butter.

They ate silently, both of them doing it more out of
necessity than real hunger. When they finished, they
quickly did the dishes and then, over more vodka, Nina
traced the route her brother would be taking on a map.

"If he did have to leave the train, he told me he would
go far north, here, to Kouvola. If anyone chased him,
he was sure he could get rid of them in the heavy forests
and over the lakes."

Carter nodded. "Makes sense. This time of year the
lakes will be frozen. He could make good time, even
overland."

"From Kouvola he would take a bus to Lahti, after
having bought a full-fare ticket to Helsinki. There he
would leave the bus and head south, overland again,
here, to Borga . . ."

She kept talking, getting more animated by the second. It was as if, by tracing the route on the map, Nina
could actually see her brother doing it, heading for
safety.

By the time she finished, she was actually excited.

"And where do we make contact?"

"There is a funeral home just outside Borga, across
the lake. Joseph knows the owner well. The man has
agreed to hide him until we arrive."

"Okay," Carter said, stretching, "let's get some
sleep. Tomorrow is going to be a long day. You can

have the bed. I'll take the sofa."

"I feel awful," she sighed. "If you don't mind, I'm going to take a bath."

She heated water while Carter made up the sofa. He heard her pour the water as he slipped out of his clothes and beneath the heavy down quilt. To his surprise, when he rolled over, Nina was removing her clothes without dimming the lantern or setting up the screen in front of the old-fashioned tub.

There was no shyness; neither was there any overt boldness.

Carter started to roll away as the sweater and jeans came off, and he felt a rising knot of expectation in his throat.

Suddenly she flashed him one quick look and a brief smile.

The hell with it, he thought, and gave himself up to the deliberate enjoyment of her body.

His impression of her had always been that of a child-woman. Nearly nude, that impression went out the window. She was small, but all woman.

Unselfconsciously and with no waste of time, Nina bent forward slightly to unhook her bra and free her breasts. Then she hooked her thumbs in her panties to shed them.

She braced a graceful hand and arm against the edge and put one foot into the tub, testing the water. From across the room, Carter could smell the woman-fragrance that comes from health and heat and activity. The soap became perfume fading into the natural fragrance of a woman's skin.

When she stood and reached for a towel, Carter could take no more. He rolled over into the sofa and clamped his eyes shut.

A few moments later, the light was extinguished and he heard her crawl into bed.

Then, "Nick?"

"Yeah?" His voice sounded as though it had come from the bottom of a barrel.

"Do you mean to tell me that you're really going to sleep on that lumpy sofa?"

"Why you . . ."

He was off the sofa and into the bed in two leaps, the last of his own words cut off by her laugh.

They came into each other's arms, and their naked flesh trembled from the contact. Nina was warm and sofa and her hard nipples were like tiny buttons against his chest. They kissed passionately, their tongues darting against one another's.

Carter broke the kiss and looked down at her. "Are you drunk or do you really know what you're doing?"

"Both," she moaned. "I wanted to do this two years ago."

He felt her body lift to his. He caressed her naked, trembling thighs as his hot mouth came down once more in search of hers. As his hand roamed, she struggled harder and harder toward his insistent caresses.

He felt her go limp. The warmth of her lips seemed to sear his as excitement lurched through his body. Trapped between his hands and his kissing mouth, she moaned with real desire.

She lay, quivering, on her back as his lips and tongue teased her tingling flesh. Her head began to roll from side to side as his kisses found her distended nipples. He bent over the soft mounds, gently loving them with his mouth. He kissed and licked them, moving from tip to tip. Her lips were half parted. The look in her eyes clearly registered her low boiling point.

He stroked and cupped the pale globes, and she felt his warm hardness pressing against her thigh as he kissed her.

His hands slid down her belly. The weight of his strong body kept her thighs apart as he probed with gentle fingers. Nina rotated her hips rhythmically in response to his expert touch.

"Enough, enough!" she cried at last.

"What?"

"I said, enough."

"Enough?" he chuckled. "After you did that number on me by the tub?"

Her eyes opened and she smiled up at him. "It worked, didn't it?"

He moved upward between her parted thighs and entered her easily.

She cried out, but it soon faded into a faint, mewling sound. Her face contorted in passion, and a light film of perspiration coated her forehead as her hair swung back and forth across her face.

There was a momentary pause, and then violence.

A howl erupted from her throat. But it was not a sound of anger or pain, more like one of victory . . . a pleasant victory over whatever devils had beleaguered her these past few hours.

As Carter made his own way toward fulfillment, Nina twitched and lurched, drawing from their union every ounce of pleasure that was in it, and at the same time inflaming his body almost beyond endurance.

Then he was at the crest, the moment all the nerves in his body concentrated their forces and brought them together between his legs.

With a throaty growl, he exploded.

And then he exploded again.

"My God," he breathed heavily, releasing her and falling breathless beside her.

They lay silent for several moments, and then his hand sneaked out to caress her. She lifted it and placed it back on his own chest.

"What's the matter?"

"Tomorrow's a rough day, remember?" she said lightly, and curled into his arm.

FIVE

The morning sun of Paris was warm, but a brisk breeze stirred the papers in the gutter. Less than ten short blocks away, the bells of Notre Dame called the faithful to early mass.

In front of the small Left Bank pension stood a black, late-model Ford Cortina sedan. It had been rented the previous evening by Gregor Leventov. Because of the necessity of time, he had rented the car with cover papers that had been issued him years before, to be used when operating abroad.

That had been his mistake, using a cover that they knew about.

That was how they had located him.

Major Anya Chevola had smelled out the plot by putting hundreds of small pieces together: a random report by a waiter at the Georgian restaurant where Shalin and

Leventov had lunched together that day; the travel reports of both of their chauffeurs; the interrogation of everyone connected with them for the last two years.

That interrogation had uncovered the third plotter: Nikolai Gusenko, head of the KGB station in Madrid.

Major Chevola had acted fast when she learned from a routine GRU report from Khodinsk that Leventov had taken a transport plane from Moscow to Paris.

She had sent a crack, four-man team to Madrid and had come to Paris herself.

Her orders before leaving Moscow were clear: "It is fairly certain now that only the three of them know about the microfilm. We must try and take them alive, if possible. If that does not prove feasible, make sure that what they know goes no further."

Now Major Anya Chevola stood in an alley between two stores, watching the pension and the car. She had been there nearly two hours and her legs were getting numb. But she had chosen the duty because she drew less attention than her male aide would have in the same spot. The sun climbed and she could feel the heat of its welcome rays on the back of her neck.

A fat woman went by wheeling a baby carriage, her body soft and shapeless, her stockings wrinkled and sagging. She saw the attractive blond woman dressed in chic black leather.

"Poule," she sniffed. "Was it such a slow night that you must foul the neighborhood at this hour of the morning?"

"Move along, you cow," Anya Chevola hissed in perfect French, and turned away.

She waited.

A delivery truck went by, milk cases rattling, leaving a trail of melted ice water in its wake.

A Paris police car came slowly by, the two patrolmen lolling in the front seat, coats unbuttoned, faces listless; they gave Anya scarcely a glance. A young housewife walked by the alley, her heels clicking on the pavement. She, too, glanced at the attractive blonde. But instead of a haughty comment, she merely smiled and shrugged.

Then the front door of the pension opened.

Anya Chevola stood rigid as Gregor Leventov shuffled down the stairs. In baggy trousers, a windbreaker, and a cloth cap, with a cigarette hanging from the side of his mouth, he looked like a Parisian workingman on his day off. He could even be departing for mass. As he stood on the curb looking up and down the street, Anya squeezed further back into the shadows.

Leventov got into his car and roared off. A black Citroen with two men in the front seat immediately pulled out from a side street. The Citroen stopped just long enough for Major Chevola to dive into the back seat.

"Keep him in sight but be careful," she said.

"When do we take him?" one of the men asked.

"When we are sure he can lead us to nothing."

They crossed the Seine and drove in what seemed like circles for a half hour.

"He's stopping."

"Drive past, slowly."

"It's the offices of Iberia."

They stopped a block away and parked.

"Yevgeny, does he know you?" Anya asked the dark-haired giant in the front passenger seat.

"No, we have never met."

"Then go into the office and try to find out what he is doing. But be careful. Don't spook him into running. An incident on the open street we can do without."

The man hopped out and sprinted toward the airline offices. Anya walked down the block and crossed the street. There was a small café right across from the Iberia offices, and it was just opening. She went inside, sat down at a table near the window, and ordered coffee.

Ten minutes later, Yevgeny came out and headed toward the Citroen. Leventov was practically right behind him, heading toward his own car. They did the same routine, and two blocks later fell in behind him.

"Why did he go to Iberia?" Anya asked.

"He verified an air delivery in Madrid this morning. Some kind of commercial cargo."

"Damn," Anya hissed from the back seat. "Let's hope they have located Gusenko."

"He's heading back to the pension."

"Take the antidote pills now," the woman said. "If it is necessary, we will use only the gas pistols."

All three popped pills into their mouths.

Leventov pulled up in front of the pension and went inside. Anya Chevola was out of the car in a flash, already running.

"One of you come behind me—the other find the rear entrance!"

A teen-age girl was behind the desk reading a magazine. Otherwise the small lobby was empty. When the girl's eyes stayed on the magazine, Anya walked right past her to the stairs.

She paused just long enough on the first landing to hear footsteps climbing above her. Once past the first floor, she sprinted. She caught up with Leventov on the fourth floor just as he was opening his door.

He turned, fast. His short, awkward appearance was deceiving. He was lithe and quick.

But before he had swung halfway around, Anya was on him. She grabbed him by the back of his collar and yanked the windbreaker down hard. At the same time, she pushed the muzzle of the gas pistol in his face.

"You know what this is, Comrade Gregor Leventov. Inside, quietly!"

She could hear Yevgeny's tread behind her. Leventov seemed to go limp. He moved into the room. The second agent arrived at the door.

"Stay outside and watch," Anya hissed, then closed the door, whirling on Leventov. "What did you send to Madrid?"

"I don't know what you're talking about."

Yevgeny hit him, open-handed, along the side of the head, his palm directly over the ear.

Leventov growled in pain and staggered across the room. Near the bed he tripped.

Too late they saw what he was doing. From beneath the pillow he pulled a silenced Stechkin, and fired as he rolled to his back.

Anya Chevola had no choice. She stepped forward and fired the gas pistol directly into Leventov's face.

The gas was instantly effective, but, just in case, she kicked the Stechkin from his grasp.

Behind her, Yevgeny groaned.

"Were you hit?" she asked over her shoulder, stooping to strip all identification from Leventov's body and slipping the Stechkin into her coat pocket.

"Yes, my arm, but it's not bleeding badly. What is that?" he asked, moving to her side and staring down at the piece of paper in her hand.

"His receipt from Iberia Airlines. He shipped a casket. Damn! They must get Gusenko before he disposes of it!"

Nikolai Gusenko entered the small café and took a table far enough from the window so he couldn't be seen from the outside. But he could see all of the street, as well as the entrance to the hotel across the street.

The café reeked of frying food. Two tables away a peasant woman sat munching bread and eating hard fried eggs so tiny each was a single mouthful.

Watching her, it occurred to Gusenko that he hadn't eaten in over twenty hours.

First there had been the flight from Paris. Then the transfer of the casket to the old truck. He himself had driven the truck out of Madrid into the Guadarrama Mountains to Avila. There, in a tiny village, he had passed the body over to a grieving trio: the mother and father, and a heartbroken fiancé, the local school-teacher, a young man Angelina Galadin had known since childhood. The fiancé had taken the news of Angelina's death very badly, and was shocked that suicide had been listed by the Soviet authorities as the cause of death. The Russians must be crazy, he thought: why couldn't they have said it was just a terrible accident with a speeding automobile?

For the first fifteen minutes of their meeting Gusenko thought that he might have to fight off the young man, who was so distraught as to be almost violent when he saw the casket. He couldn't believe that he'd lost Angelina forever. He thought back to that wonderful, passion-filled long weekend they had spent in Paris only a few months before. She would have been home soon for good . . . they were to be married . . . and now . . .

On and on he went, his anguish heart-rending, the old couple standing numb behind him.

At last Gusenko took the weeping young man aside, had him sign a receipt, and offered his condolences.

The casket was transferred to, of all things, a horse-drawn cart, and Gusenko watched them wind their way into the rocky hills. They would return to their tiny village and bury her and mourn together.

Gusenko had then driven to the train station in the walled city of Avila, where he abandoned the truck. It had been purchased weeks before in Madrid, using a fictitious name so it could never be traced.

From Avila he had trained north to Segovia. In Segovia he had called the hotel, and got his first shock.

She had not checked in.

She had not wanted to go to France on holiday in the first place. Had she just not come? Surely not. Surely she would have left him a message.

Carmela Savona had been Gusenko's mistress for two years, nearly all the time he had been posted in Spain. It was she who carried the false passports and other papers that would allow them to disappear for days, even weeks, if necessary, until the turbulence in Moscow settled down and Gusenko could come out of hiding.

And she had the car. He had no means of getting a car here in Segovia.

Where was the bitch?

"Señor?"

A waiter set a stained menu in front of Gusenko and rubbed his greasy hands on an already filthy apron. The Russian was again reminded that for many hours he had taken no food.

But food was not what he needed.

"You have vodka?"

"Sí, señor."

"Bring me vodka."

The drink bucked him up a little. But not much.

Again he phoned the hotel. "No, señor, I am sorry. But we have no Señorita Savona registered."

He ordered another drink, and another. He sat over the table, a huge man, hunched and morose, liquor and lack of sleep giving an added fierceness to his deep-set eyes, making him look older than his thirty-odd years.

He sat drinking for two more hours, until he finally admitted to himself that Carmela Savona was not coming.

He would have to run by himself. He had his own passport and papers, but he dared not use them to leave the country. He would have to hide in Spain.

Where? he asked his vodka-fogged mind.

Bilbao. He had spent a week there last year by the seashore. He had money, enough to buy himself anonymity for a few days. He hoped that would be long enough.

He threw bills on the table to pay for the vodka, and

walked into the sunlight. Buses, carts, and small trucks buzzed around him like angry hornets, their motors roaring, the constant blare of their horns adding to the noisy bustle.

It was market day, and chaos.

Gusenko remembered seeing the sign for the central bus terminus, and headed that way.

He was just turning off the Calle Vallejo into the Plaza San Esteban, when he saw the car rock to a halt a block in front of him. It was long and sleek, with its black paint shining in the sunlight.

There were tinted side and rear windows; one could see out but not in. In the front seat, two men sat watching him.

They were in the mountains. It was winter, with a chilling wind rushing through the plaza. But beneath his heavy coat, his sweater, and the rest of his winter wear, Gusenko could feel sweat ooze from every pore of his big body.

He dropped to one knee and retied a shoelace. From that position he sneaked a look behind him.

A second car, the same style and make, blocked the entrance to the plaza.

It was then that Gusenko knew that Carmela Savona was never coming. He had been so careful, so sure that his KGB comrades didn't have a hint of his Spanish liaison.

He had been wrong.

And chances were good that Carmela Savona had paid for her lover's mistake with her life.

Gusenko stood, forcing his feet to take him past the car. As he drew abreast, the door opened. Two men swung directly in front of him.

"Get in the car, comrade." The man who spoke offered his hand as if in greeting. It held a small pistol.

Gusenko stood, rooted, his drink-fogged mind trying

to reason an escape. From his left some women, all wearing dark head scarves and black, worn clothing, stepped from the sidewalk. All of them carried large shopping baskets. They had already seen the confrontation and their eyes were bright with anticipation.

Gusenko had been in Spain long enough to know the reason for their anticipation. He was dressed as their men would be dressed, in the heavy woolens and worn, manure-stained boots of a Spanish workingman.

He moved toward them, shouting over his shoulder at the two by the car, "Why can't the Guardia leave me alone? What do you want with me? I am a simple man. I have done nothing. Why do the police hound me?"

The two bulky KGB agents moved toward him. Behind them, across the street, Gusenko saw a bus preparing to leave, maneuvering out into traffic.

Thirty yards and he would be safe. A hundred street peddlers lined the plaza with their stands, reducing traffic to a crawl . . . except for the monstrous buses. By the time the cars could turn around and escape the plaza, he would be dropping off the bus a mile away.

He was close enough to the women to smell their sweat and cheap scent.

"Go on, señor, run!" one of the women suddenly shrilled.

The larger of the KGB men dived for Gusenko. The woman, shrieking, threw her basket between his legs, effectively tripping him.

Gusenko ran, butting his shoulder into the second man, knocking him out of the way.

The bus was roaring away now, kicking up a dust cloud from its heavy tires. It was one of those old-fashioned buses still used in Spain, with an open rear door so that it barely had to stop to pick up passengers on the narrow mountain roads. It just slowed and the people swung aboard.

But the door was on the other side.

Gusenko slowed. The rear of the bus passed him and he sped up.

He was going to make it.

He came around the bus, sweat pouring into his eyes. There was a woman's scream.

Another bus was barreling into the square on the other side.

Gusenko himself screamed. He was inches in front of the huge front bumper and the driver couldn't even see him.

The world burst into flaming pain. He felt himself being carried around and around as the big tires mangled his body.

The sun was spinning. He no longer had size or shape. He was nothing, with the sound of screaming brakes and roaring engines in his ears.

But through it all, one last thought rose in his mind: *This was it, the sick thing that all men dread.*

And, after all, it became such a small thing to die.

SIX

Light streamed into the room through the cracks around the thin, cheap curtains. Yawning, Carter sat up and checked his watch on the night table.

Nine o'clock. More than enough time to get to Borga and rent the car.

He lit a cigarette and studied the body sprawled beside him. The quilt had slipped down, exposing one pert breast. The rest of her body was twisted in such a grotesque position that, had it been any body but a dancer's, Carter would have thought her in pain.

He leaned over, tugged the quilt a little lower, and tickled her flat belly. Nina moaned and pushed his hand away. In so doing, the quilt slipped even further.

It was a nice body, all warmly pink, gently curved, with hips strong and fatless, and lovely breasts that didn't tilt up or down.

She sighed, still in sleep, and turned on her side, facing him. Again, Carter reached forward and tickled the breast closest to him.

She squinted one eye and said, very clearly, "I may just punch you in the nose."

"That's not a very romantic way to start the day."

She opened both eyes and scowled at the sunlight invading the room. Then her eyes grew wide, and Carter smiled. He had the idea that she was just remembering what had happened the night before.

He said so.

"Maybe," she purred, and stretched, kicking the quilt the rest of the way off. "What time is it?"

"Early."

"Then where are you going?"

"Borga, to rent the car."

Nina grabbed his shoulders and tugged him back to the bed. "You said it was early."

With those words, she set about reigniting the previous night's fire.

It didn't take long.

"Car, got to get the car," Carter sighed, but his words lacked conviction.

Their bodies met with an even greater intensity than the night before. Their breathing came in short gasps until, at the climax, there was no one else in the whole world but the two of them, with the northern sunlight streaming through the window.

When it was over, reality set back in all too soon. They dressed quietly and Carter headed for the door.

"I'll be back in a couple of hours. Be ready."

She nodded, and he set off around the lake.

Borga was a good-sized town, large enough that no eyebrows were raised when an American wished to rent a car for a two-week period. There was no problem with his desire to return the car in Helsinki, only a drop-off charge.

The car would actually be dropped off much farther north, at Kauliranta, on the Swedish frontier.

He spotted them about the same time they spotted him, just as he was coming out of the car rental office. They were walking along the sidewalk directly opposite him, two of them, wearing jeans the same as everybody else.

But their shirts were different. Nearly every man Carter had met that day wore checked, heavy hunting shirts. It was that kind of an area. Under their coats, these two wore white dress shirts.

For the next half hour, Carter edged in and out of stores. They followed his direction for only a short time and then disappeared.

Perhaps it was just his imagination, he thought, and retraced his steps back to the car.

He took a different road around the lake, and back-tracked several times.

No sign of them.

The Killmaster put it down to his usual paranoia about detection on a delicate mission, and drove to the cabin. By the time he had arrived, it was midafternoon and the long winter night had already descended.

Nina was drinking coffee and pacing the tiny cabin like a caged lioness.

"Anything outside while I was gone?"

"What do you mean?"

"Anybody been around?"

"No. At least I didn't see anyone. Why?"

"Nothing," Carter said, bending to extinguish the fire.

The funeral home was on the lake about four miles from the center of Borga. There was a high ledge surrounding a good part of the grounds. The main building was set well back. It was sprawling and large. Other smaller buildings squatted in deeper shadow.

Carter parked in the wide turnaround in front of the building and killed the engine. "If he isn't here . . . ?"

"We come back tomorrow. And if not then, the day after," Nina replied, a solid set to her chin.

"Okay," Carter said with a shrug. "Let's go."

They approached the wide doorway. There was an aura of stillness about the place, only the low hum of some kind of machine from one of the outbuildings and the chirping of a bird in the vacuumlike silence.

There was a woman at the desk just inside the door, fortyish, stern, with lips turned downward in practiced mourning. She said nothing, merely nodded as they approached the desk.

Nina did the talking. "We are the Swensons, here for the viewing of my uncle."

A little fire came into the woman's eyes. Wordlessly, she directed them down a long hall and punched the button of an intercom on her desk.

Nina's grip on Carter's arm was like a vise. "He's here, Nick! He's here!"

"Just how sure is Joseph of these people?"

"Very sure. Two of their relatives died in the Caucasus some time ago. Joseph was instrumental in cutting a lot of red tape so the bodies could be returned. They were very grateful."

They entered a large sitting room. Another woman sat at the far end. She was dressed in a simple but elegant black dress and was an amazingly beautiful woman, with dark red lips and warm brown eyes. As they approached, she uncrossed her legs and stood.

"I am Helga Nordstrom. This way, please."

They went down another long hall, past viewing rooms to a pair of stout, wooden doors.

"The room is completely private. You have fifteen minutes, twenty at the most."

They entered and the door closed behind them. A flower-bedecked casket was on a raised dais in the center of the room. One half of the lid was open and the corpse of an old man was visible to the waist.

Carter felt a tremor go through Nina as she looked at the body, and then another as a pair of drapes parted and a man stepped into the room.

"Joseph . . ."

She was across the room and into her brother's arms like a shot. After lots of hugs and kisses and tears, she broke free and introduced Carter.

"Thank you so very much for helping me," Kadinskov said, pressing Carter's outstretched hand between his own.

The Killmaster shrugged it off. He wanted very much to question Nina's brother about the details of his escape, as well as the KGB connection that led up to it, but it didn't look like there would be time.

"The woman said twenty minutes. What happens then?"

Kadinskov drew a crudely drawn map from his pocket. "He"—he nodded toward the casket—"is being taken to the church of Hattula . . . here. About halfway, we will enter these woods. There is a logging camp, here, about a mile off the main road. Nordstrom's driver will drop me there."

"And that's where we pick you up?" Carter asked.

"Yes. There is a sign on the main road for the logging camp. You can't miss it."

Carter thought for a moment. "Why can't you just leave with us from here?"

"I don't want to involve the Nordstroms any further. Just in case you have been followed, or they somehow may have spotted me, I want to keep these people in the clear. What they have already done is very dangerous for them."

Carter nodded. "One more thing. Why did you take the alternate plan, leave the train?"

"It was just as I feared. The KGB never lives up to their promises."

Tersely, he reiterated what he had done in Moscow

for Leventov, and the subsequent try for him on the train.

"What did you sew into the woman's belly?"

"A small package. I don't know what was in it."

"The woman's name?"

"I don't know that, either. I do know that the woman was Spanish, and the body was being transported to Madrid, back to her family for burial."

Not much to go on, the Killmaster thought, but he stored the details in his memory bank anyway, in case Kadinskov's information might one day prove useful.

The door opened and Helga Nordstrom's beautiful head popped through. "It is time, you must go."

It was pitch-black, not a light for miles around, and the moon was long gone under heavy, flying clouds. Beside him, Nina held the crude map in the light of the dash.

"Fork ahead," Carter said.

"Yes," she replied. "Take the center one. That's the road that will take us all the way through the forest."

The road turned to gravel just after they entered the woods. Here and there were smaller private roads. Through the blackness Carter could make out names painted on rustic signs, and occasionally a summer cottage tucked away in the trees beside a dark lake.

"It should be five miles exactly from here," Nina said, "on the right. Check the odometer."

"Got it," Carter said, nodding.

The words were scarcely out of his mouth when a pair of headlights appeared behind them, coming fast. Until now they had only seen a few cars on the lonely stretch of highway, and all of them had been going the other way, toward Helsinki.

Carter was about to slow and let the car pass, when one of the headlights veered to his left and came on like a shot.

Motorcycle, he thought, and then it flew by them and

disappeared around the next curve.

Carter sped up and the second motorcycle dropped back. He slowed, but still the light behind him faded.

"What's wrong?" Nina asked, noting the frown on his forehead.

"Motorcycles."

"What about them?"

"Why did a pair of them come up on us and then split apart?"

Her eyes grew wide in the dashboard lights. "Us?"

Carter shrugged. "We'll see."

The road climbed steadily and wound like a moving snake. About two miles farther on, he looked down and to his left. Again there were two lights.

No way, he thought, for the first one to get back by him. There were now three of them.

Then he saw the bobbing glow of a taillight in the distance ahead.

They were pacing him and Nina.

"There it is . . . the sign!"

Carter had already seen it. When they drew abreast of it, he killed his lights and gunned the engine. The car flew ahead and Nina started shouting.

"You passed it! Back there, the sign for the logging camp!"

"I know. Trust me."

It didn't take a genius to figure it out. He had been tagged right from the beginning—tagged and then trailed all the way across Europe. They had probably used teams, making them almost impossible for Carter to spot.

It had already gotten through to Nina. "The motorcycles?"

Carter nodded. "Yeah, most likely a crack assassination team. They've probably already guessed that we're down to the wire . . . somewhere tonight we're meeting your brother."

Since they had passed the sign, they had already

passed another road, and Carter could see a break in the trees ahead indicating a third. They were all on the right, and the entrances were laid over with undisturbed snow.

It wouldn't be difficult for the bad guys to figure out which one they took.

Carter reached the road, braked, and spun the car off. He went about twenty yards, stopped, and shifted into reverse to wait.

It didn't take long. He could hear the roar of their engines and then, when they spotted the tracks, he could hear them throttling down.

"What are you going to do?" Nina whispered.

"Make 'em guess . . . at first," Carter said. "And then make 'em play on my turf."

The engines died. Carter did a one-thousand count to ten, and dropped the clutch.

The little car took off like a jackrabbit backward. The instant the rear wheels hit the road, he spun the wheel and hit the lights.

One of them was off his bike, slinging a machine pistol over his shoulder. The second was still sitting on his machine, his helmet off, a walkie-talkie up to his mouth.

In the glare of the car's lights, Carter and Nina could both recognize the face.

"Henri Duval!" Nina gasped. "From Milan . . . the ballet!"

"Duval my ass," Carter growled, shifting into first. "I'll bet he speaks perfect Russian."

The car lurched ahead. Both men dived for the trees.

Carter meant to cream both machines. At the last second he lost traction in the snow and only managed to get one.

"That should hold them for a little bit, until their buddy catches up," he hissed.

They must have broken Nina's cover some time ago.

Then, when they decided to use Joseph for one of their games, they sent Duval/Whoever in to spot Nina and make sure they got Joseph if he managed to slip them.

Carter told Nina as much and, white-faced, she nodded in agreement.

Around the curve, he kept his lights on, searching for the next road. When they hit it, he turned in and very carefully reversed back out in the same tracks.

It was nearly a mile further to the logging camp road. Carter hit it full tilt, and charged up it under an umbrella of tall, leafless trees. One hundred, two hundred, three hundred yards of narrow, winding road . . . and nothing.

"Come on, come on!" he hissed. "Where the hell . . ."

And then they burst into a huge clearing and Carter began snapping the lights off and on.

Except for a couple of big logging trucks and a bulldozer, the place looked abandoned and ghostly. There were several buildings leaning as if they would wobble and fall over in the next big storm.

In less than two minutes Carter had crisscrossed and spun the car around the clearing several times, making a mess of his own tracks.

Then he spun the car around and backed it under a wooden overhead. He killed the lights and engine, and jumped out. Nina was right behind him, calling to her brother.

"Up here!"

They looked. He was half in, half out of a second-story window, a handgun glinting at the end of both arms.

"We're blown!" Carter shouted. "Get down here!"

Lithely, Kadinskov dropped to the ground and ran to join them. "What is it?"

"They had Nina fingered, probably trailed us all the way from Milan. Chances are their job was to take you out if their agent on the train missed.''

"How many?''

"Three, on motorcycles. Nina, you drive. Joseph, in the passenger seat.''

"What are you going to do?'' Nina asked, her brother already climbing into the car.

"Lead them away from the road.''

"No, Nick, you've got to come with us!'' she cried.

He ignored her. "You've got papers to get you to Italy. You know where to pick up new papers there. I'll buy you time here.''

Suddenly she was against him, her lips pressed to his. "Thank you, Nick.''

He practically shoved her into the driver's seat.

"Don't start the engine until you hear the first shot. When you do, go like hell, hit the road, and don't look back. Joseph, take good care of her.''

"I will. And . . . thank you.''

Carter turned and ran down the lane as fast as his legs would carry him, unholstering Wilhelmina.

A hundred yards short of the road he heard the engines. At fifty he heard them cut off, and hit the trees. Ten yards in, he stopped and dropped into a crouch.

It could have been an hour. Actually, it was about two minutes.

The snow was about a foot deep with a hard crust on top. It was impossible for them to be quiet. They were easy to spot by sound. One man was leading point, near the lane, on Carter's side. The other two were about twenty yards behind him, one on each side of the road.

Carter narrowed his eyes, straining them in the darkness.

And then he saw him, his helmet discarded, coming upright, the muzzle of his machine pistol moving from side to side.

Carter was on one knee, motionless, the Luger straight out from his shoulder in both hands.

He waited until the man was less than ten yards from him, and fired twice.

All three machine pistols barked at the same time, one in the air as the dying man fell, and the other two in Carter's direction.

But he was already flat on the ground, his eyes darting around a rotten log.

They were moving as they fired, trying to outflank him.

Then the firing stopped and all of them, hunter and hunted alike, heard the car roaring down the lane.

The two men reacted fast. One of them fired short bursts in Carter's direction to hold him down while the other sprinted back toward the road to head off the car.

Carter could not see either of them, nor could he hear them now over the chaos. He did hear the car hit high gear and then hurtle around the last bend and straighten out for its run to the road.

Both men forgot about Carter now and tried to find the range on the car.

Then Nina showed her guts. She turned on the headlights. They illuminated one of the men dead center in the road. He was just bringing up his machine pistol when Carter emptied the rest of Wilhelmina's clip into him.

Five seconds later Nina hit him, sending his lifeless body into the trees. The car went on, veered into the road, rocked dangerously, and was gone.

Across the lane, Carter could hear the last man running for the road himself. The Killmaster guessed he was heading for the place where they had hidden the motorcycles.

Jamming a fresh clip into the butt of the Luger, Carter darted through the trees, pretty sure that the third man had figured out the whole scam.

When he heard the man kick the machine to life, he broke from the trees and ran full out. He was certain his prey would be intent on the car now, and could care less about who the shooter in the trees had been or where he was.

The Killmaster hit the end of the lane just as the bike roared out of the trees to his left. He got off two shots, both wild, and dived out of the way.

A stump just below the surface of the snow hit the barrel of the Luger, knocking it from his grasp. He rolled to the side just as the bike swung around and came for him.

It was Duval, and the machine pistol was slung over his shoulder. At that point, Duval wasn't interested in Carter. He wanted the occupants of the car that was long gone down the road.

Carter got to his feet just as the machine got to him. He treated the handlebars as if they were the horns of a charging bull and went right over the top of them, managing to get his arms around Duval's head and his shoulder in the man's face.

And that's the way they sailed, crazily, down the road, before the front wheel hit a slick spot and the bike went over.

Carter went to the side, sliding into the snow on his chest. Duval managed to get his leg from beneath the skidding machine and roll free. He was just unslinging the machine pistol when Carter hit him at the knees in a flying block. With a howl of pain, Duval went down and the gun went sliding across the road to disappear in a snowbank.

They were both up and at each other at once. Carter sidestepped, but Duval countered, getting his arms around the Killmaster's middle.

The intent was obvious. If he could get his hands high enough and keep his body low, he could snap Carter's spine like a twig.

Around and around they danced, suddenly tripping over the still-running motorcycle lying in the middle of the road on its side. Carter managed to keep his balance as the other man rolled free. On the way down, Carter brought his knee up into Duval's face.

It didn't put him out, but it made him good and fuzzy.

They were on opposite sides of the purring motorcycle. Carter was on his knees, waiting. When Duval started coming for him again, Carter reached out and locked his fingers behind the other man's neck. Then he pulled down, jamming Duval's face into the red-hot muffler.

His sudden screams of pain filled the night. Carter held him against the muffler with the weight of his body until he was sure the man was mad with pain.

Then he released him and waited.

When Duval struggled to his feet, still screaming, Carter brought his right hand up to the man's mangled throat. He found the Adam's apple with his fingers, and applied all his strength.

Carter felt the throat give inward, and when the screams of pain ebbed to a hoarse death rattle, he dropped him.

He took a full five minutes to get his breath and check his own injuries. Then he dragged the body into the trees.

The motorcycle, on its wheels again, was drivable. He put it on the kickstand and used the headlight to find his Luger.

One last check for debris and he was riding south toward Helsinki.

An hour later, at the main highway, he paused before turning south. His eyes flickered to the north.

They would be in Kauliranta dumping the car at about the same time he got to Helsinki. And about the time he got back to Washington, they would be disappearing somewhere into the Italian countryside.

He hoped they would find a little peace in the rest of their lives.

SEVEN

Washington, D.C., The present

When the head of AXE, David Hawk, said jump, everyone in the agency moved, fast. Nick Carter was no different.

The big man got right to it the moment Carter settled into a chair.

"This tape came over from the CIA early this morning. It was taken over the phone in Mexico City last night. Give a listen."

Hawk punched a button on a console behind his desk, and two large speakers came to life.

"I will answer no questions. I am assuming all calls to your office are taped. Please listen only. My name is Sergei Anatolyevich Tilkoff. For five years, until his un-

timely death, I was personal aide to General Ivor Yuryevich Shalin. During that time I was privy to much of
the general's work. For the past two and one half years I
have been assistant *rezident*, KGB, Soviet embassy,
Mexico City. Two months ago I fled the embassy and
went into hiding. I am sure that you can check all of the
above . . ."

Hawk hit another button and the tape stopped. "We
checked with our people in Moscow. He is what he
says."

Carter nodded and the tape continued.

"I am now in the United States. I wish to defect. For
your cooperation in resettling me with funds and a new
identity, I have information very valuable to the West.
This information concerns the so-called Andropov file.
If you are interested, please give me a number in
Washington I can call in one hour."

Hawk killed the tape. "You know the rumors?"

Carter nodded. "Like our own Mr. Hoover, Andropov had the sword of personal information to hang
over his comrades' heads. A lot of people speculated
that the information was stolen just before or just after
he died. We've dug, they've dug, but nothing has ever
turned up."

Hawk ground his teeth over a smelly cigar and
thought out loud. "According to this Tilkoff, the files
were very real and they are still missing. He was passed
on to Washington. This is the second tape."

"This is Sergei Tilkoff. Are you recording?"

Another voice, faint: "Yes."

"The Andropov file was stolen by a cabal of three
men: General Shalin, Gregor Leventov, and Nikolai
Gusenko. The file is still intact. Information concerning
this file is what I intend trading for a new life. If you are
interested, I will meet with one agent and only one
agent, alone, the day after tomorrow, at a place called

Bayou Center. It is forty miles north of New Iberia, Louisiana, on the Bayou Teche. Should you agree, there is one other stipulation. I insist that the agent I meet with be Nicholas Carter. If there is any objection to this, I think Mr. Carter will agree if I mention the name Nina Kovich, and the fact that Kovich was changed to Cavetti.

"I will expect your answer in the personals column of *The Times-Picayune* the day after tomorrow. It should read, 'Sam, all is forgiven. Come home. Lily.' "

The line was disconnected and Hawk killed the tape.

"This Nina Cavetti mean anything to you?"

"Yeah," Carter replied, "lots." He explained.

"You have interesting vacations," Hawk said dryly when Carter had finished.

"I filed a report, but I doubt if it was red-flagged."

"Do you have any idea where this Nina Cavetti and her brother are now?"

"Somewhere in Italy, I suppose. When we split in Finland that night, I figured they rated some peace and quiet."

"Why do you suppose this guy mentioned her name?"

Carter lit a cigarette and concentrated. "Probably to prove to me he was on the inside. Cavetti was the name she had with the ballet. It was her cover when she had the plastic surgery and dropped Kovich."

Hawk leaned back in his chair and lit a fresh cigar. "Any idea why this guy wants the meet with you as the go-between?"

Carter shrugged. "None, unless my name was familiar to him on their computers."

Hawk mulled this over before he spoke. "Could be, I suppose. In any event, the thinkers have decided that if this guy is for real, it might be valuable stuff."

"I thought we decided a long time ago that the Andropov file was only rumor, disinformation.''

"We did, but as somebody once said, leave no damned stone unturned. Take a shot at him, Nick. We'll handle the newspaper thing.''

"Okay." Carter stood.

"Get an open line, twenty-four-hour number from Bateman on your way out. If this Tilkoff has good stuff, I'll have someone on that line for evaluation who can tell you how much we'll pay for it.''

"Will do." Carter headed for the door.

"And, Nick . . .''

"Yeah?"

"Check the files and familiarize yourself with those three VIPs he mentioned on the tape.''

Carter took the elevator down to Records, entered the computer section, and found Howard Schmidt's assistant, Al Garrett.

"To what do I owe this esteemed honor?" Garrett growled.

"Your sweet disposition, Al," Carter said, pulling a legal pad across the desk and applying a pen to it. "Get me everything you can on these jokers. And do me a favor—dig deep.''

"Don't I always?"

Carter left Garrett's cubicle and made a beeline to the coffee machine. Then, cup in hand, he collared one of the pool operators.

"Julie, isn't it?"

"Yes, I'm flattered you remember.''

He smiled. "Names, faces, and figures; I don't forget. Do me a favor?''

"Name it."

"Bring up my file. I'm looking for a specific report I filed in the first two weeks of February 1984.''

Her fingers flew like magic over the keyboard, and the screen in front of them came to life. Dates flew by faster than Carter could catch them.

"Wait . . . too far. Back up."

She retreated, day by day, until Carter called a halt. "Hold it. That's the one. Can I have a printout?"

"You know you can't take it out of here."

"I know, darlin'. I'll shred it before I leave."

She printed out the report, had Carter sign for it, and he found a vacant desk.

As he read, it all washed back over him. He'd never tried a trace; there had been no need. And since no word of bodies matching Joseph's and Nina's descriptions had ever turned up in the international grapevine, Carter had always assumed they had made it and were living happily ever after.

He reached for the phone and dialed the in-house operator who handled agency-to-agency high-priority calls on a scrambler line.

Carter gave her his security clearance number and asked for Italian CID personnel division in Rome.

It didn't take long.

"Salvatore Mandetti. What can I do for you?"

"I'd like current status and whereabouts on one of your agents, Luigi Corelli."

"Can you hold?"

"Of course."

He was back the length of a cigarette later. "Corelli, Luigi Anto—"

"That's my man."

"Disability retirement six months ago."

"Any idea where he is now?"

"Not really. We don't keep track of personnel once they leave the service. Wait a minute . . . his checks are sent to a local post office box in Livorno. Does that help?"

"Maybe. You have a resident there?"

"No, too small, actually. I can put a request through

to the local post office there for an address and number."

"Do that, will you? And pipe it back here when you have it."

"Certainly."

Carter disconnected, shredded his file, and headed back to Al Garrett.

"Got anything?"

Garrett handed him three printouts, and Carter returned to the vacant desk. He read through all three of the files quickly, then did a reread, making notes. He was correlating the notes when the loudspeaker boomed his name.

"Nick Carter, line seven . . . Carter, pick up line seven, please."

"Yeah, Carter here."

"Hawk, Nick. The Tilkoff calls came through from Baton Rouge, both of them."

"It figures that he'd be within driving distance of the meeting place."

"And we got a rundown on this place, Bayou Center."

"Yeah?"

"It's a combination café and bait shop with cabins and boats to rent to fishermen. A widow runs it, Loretta Ducaine. It's bayou country, Nick, lonesome and tricky. Watch yourself."

"I always do," Carter chuckled. "Al got me a rundown on Tilkoff's three names."

"And?"

"A lot of similarities. Shalin was about as close to Andropov as anyone could get on the way up. At one time or another, both Gusenko and Leventov worked directly with or for Shalin before they climbed on up the ladder."

"Fits so far," Hawk said.

"And all three of them died within twenty-four hours of each other . . . and within a day of Andropov's death."

Hawk emitted a low whistle. "Now it sounds very promising. Could this Tilkoff have gotten his hands on the Andropov files and hidden them all this time?"

"Anything is possible. We'll know soon enough. I'll contact you from Louisiana."

The line went dead and Carter headed for the elevators.

EIGHT

It was Delta out of Washington into Baton Rouge, with a change of planes in Atlanta. The drive through the bayou country to New Iberia was supposed to be fifty-five minutes, but it took nearly two hours. From there it was another hour over roads that were little more than country lanes to Bayou Center.

It looked shabby, crushed by age and the damp of the surrounding area. There were two old-style, tank-top gas pumps in front of a gray shack that served as the station, café, and bait shop.

A faded Coca-Cola sign over the door gave him the name B YOU CE TER. Behind the shack were some weatherbeaten frame cabins and a boathouse with a float pier extending out into the river. A thermometer by the door read 102.

Nobody was in sight. Carter hit the battered screen door and walked in. It was cooler inside, away from the direct impact of the late-afternoon sun. There was a Coke machine, a cigarette machine, a battered cash register, and a glass-topped counter, thick with dust, containing cans of oil, sunglasses, candy bars, and spark plugs.

Along the back wall was a greasy grill fronted by a six-stool counter. A scrawled sign yellow with grease and grime declared ham hocks and beans as the special of the day. Carter guessed the day was somewhere during World War II.

"Anybody here?"

An old man shambled from the rear through a pair of curtains that served as a doorway. He was munching on the remnants of a sandwich, and looked as if he'd passed through an autopsy room and survived.

"Yeah?" He barely glanced at Carter.

"Can I get a cabin for the night?"

"Loretta, fella wants a cabin."

He passed by Carter and the screen door slammed behind him. The curtains parted again, and an Amazon with jet-black hair going in every direction stepped through. She wore a second skin of jeans and a peasant-type blouse with no bra. The blouse's scoop neckline was cut low, and Carter could see the deep, smooth cleft between her breasts, tanned all the way down. There was some excitement in the way she breathed, but not much.

"How many nights?" Her voice was low, cigarette husky, and the twang was pure Cajun.

"What?"

"The cabin . . . how many nights?"

Carter shrugged. "One, maybe two. If you're not full."

This was greeted with a healthy laugh. "Shit. Sign the book."

"The book" was a dog-eared ledger with names and dates scrawled indiscriminately across the pages.

Carter signed his name carefully, and the date.

"First night in advance. Twenty bucks."

"Add a beer to that."

"Another buck, cooler's right there."

Carter dropped a dollar on top of the twenty and got the beer. The bills went into a cigar box behind the café counter.

He sat on a stool. "I'm supposed to meet a couple of other guys here . . . maybe do some fishing. Name's Carter—anybody leave a message for me?"

"Nah, no message." Her black eyes looked him up and down. "You don't look the fisherman type."

"I'm just learning."

Up close she looked better, with the wild darkness of the bayous in her eyes. When she spoke she leaned forward over the counter. Her mouth was wide, her lower lip full and sensuous, and her unsupported breasts filled the open gap in the blouse.

Carter finished the beer, keeping his eyes above her neck. "Well, I think I'll get out of these city clothes. Which cabin?"

She dropped a key on the counter. "Number four. It's the one with a view, right on the river."

"Thanks," Carter said, picking up the key and heading for the door.

"Hey . . ."

"Yeah?"

"You a cop?"

Carter chuckled. "Hardly." He slammed the door behind him and headed for the cabin.

He didn't need the key: the lock didn't work.

The cabin wasn't much to look at. Sunlight sifted through cracks in the walls and dotted a frayed hooked rug spread over a warped pine floor. The walls were half logs chinked with plaster, and the ceiling was bare rafters with last year's wasp nests in the corners.

There was no television and no air conditioner. The bed was old, with brass pipe framing. A battered armchair, a dresser with the veneer curling at the edges, and a wooden chair were the furnishings.

Mildew touched all of it with damp fingers.

Carter checked the shower. It worked.

He stripped and took a long one using only the cold tap. He didn't bother to towel down. It wouldn't do any good. In the heat he would be soaking wet again in ten minutes.

He unpacked, leaving the Luger and the stiletto in the false bottom of the suitcase, and stretched naked on the bed.

He dozed fitfully, and came awake at the sound of knocking on the door. The beams of sunlight had disappeared from the cracks in the walls and the break in the curtains.

He had slept longer than he intended.

Just as he rolled out of the bed, the door opened and she stepped into the room. It took all of four seconds for her to take in every pore and hair of his body, then she spoke. "Telephone call for ya, long distance."

"Thanks."

He was sure she was smiling when she turned and left.

He pulled on a shirt and a pair of khakis, and walked up to the main building. She was drinking a beer at the counter.

"Phone's there on the wall."

"Yeah, Carter here."

"How's the bayou?" The voice was low, sultry, with a slight southern twang. It belonged to David Hawk's chief assistant, Ginger Bateman.

"Hot," Carter replied. "What have you got?"

"He called again."

"And?"

"Evidently he's got someone spotting you. He knew what time you got in and he knows your cabin number."

"Figures," Carter said, eyeing the raven-haired woman at the counter who was in turn eyeing him.

"About four miles above you, on Bayou Teche Road, there's a dive called Grady's. You're supposed to be there around ten o'clock. Park, go in, and have a few drinks. Stay exactly an hour and then leave."

"Is that it?"

"That's it."

"Jesus," Carter growled. "Anything else?"

"You got a request reply from Italian CID, a guy named Mandetti."

"Yeah, on Luigi Corelli," he replied, almost dismissing it as irrelevent now.

"No forward from P.O. Box Livorno re Corelli. His mail is picked up."

"Okay, it's really not important anyway. I'll check in tomorrow."

"Right."

Carter hung up and ambled to the counter. "Thanks for taking the call. How about a couple of burgers and some fries?"

"Burgers, yeah. Fries, no. Fryer's broke."

"Oh. Just the burgers then."

Carter got a beer while she cooked. When she slid the plate toward him, she moved up onto the stool beside him.

"You don't look like the fisherman type."

"You already told me that," Carter growled, washing the greasy burger down with beer.

"But you do look like a cop."

"Look, lady, you also mentioned that before. And I'll tell you again, I'm not a cop."

She shrugged and lit a cigarette. "I hope not. It's very

unhealthy in this part of the bayou for cops."

She slid off the stool and disappeared behind the curtained doorway.

Carter finished the food, cursing Tilkoff for choosing such a place for a meet.

Carter took his bag from the lockless cabin and put it in the trunk of the car when he left.

Other than a single light in one of the other cabins and the neon in front of the place, there was no sign of anything living. Bayou Center was closed up for the night.

He drove north, four miles by the odometer.

Grady's wasn't hard to find. He could see the lights and hear the thumping beat of a country-and-western band from a hundred yards away.

He parked the rented Pontiac in the middle of a few dozen pickup trucks and walked through a long, blue-lit tunnel. Through a door at the end of it he entered a sewer, upholstered in red with a number of tables in the rear around a small bandstand and a bar in front.

A few bearded faces turned his way as he moved to the bar and found a stool.

While he waited, he took in the room. Standard dress was T-shirt or checkered shirt and jeans for both men and women. That was why his eye found Loretta Ducaine so easily. She was at a table near the bandstand with two of the biggest and meanest dudes Carter had ever seen, and she had shed the jeans and peasant blouse. She was now wearing a red dress that looked as if it were painted on with nothing but skin underneath. It covered everything but hid nothing.

She returned his look with one of her own that could kill. Carter turned back as the bartender returned.

"Five bucks."

Carter didn't question it. He dropped a twenty on the

bar and sipped the beer. It was warm.

Twenty minutes passed and the band took a break. Carter ordered another beer.

"Make it two, Grady."

She slipped onto the stool beside him and her perfume fanned out to fill his nostrils.

"Hi," Carter said, pushing a ten across to pay for the two beers.

"My friends would like to meet you."

He swiveled his head around. The two giants were sitting back in their chairs, about six feet of legs stretched in front of them.

"No, thanks. I'm just going to have a couple of beers and hit the sack."

She sipped the beer and started peeling the label with a long, red nail.

"Look, sweetie, let's say you're not a cop. I'm starting to believe you. But my friends there, well, they ain't so sure. They'd like a little chat with you, just to make sure."

Carter started to boil. He took one more look at the two men and then turned back to her.

"Loretta . . . it is Loretta, isn't it?"

"Yeah, it's Loretta."

"Well, look, Loretta, I got business around here, yes. And it has nothing to do with your Mississippi Mafia over there. I don't want to talk to them and I don't want to talk to you. I just want to have a couple of beers and go back to bed."

"My friends won't like that."

"Fuck your friends."

That did it. She slid off the stool and went back to the table.

Carter nursed the beer until the clock behind the bar was standing straight up, eleven o'clock.

"Can I buy a bottle?"

"Sure. Twenty-five bucks."

Carter paid, and grasped the sacked bottle by the neck as he walked back out of the tunnel.

They were waiting by his car, both bearded giants leaning against the trunk and a third a few steps to the right with a sawed-off baseball bat.

"My friends and me, we'd like to see some kind of identification, friend."

Carter smiled. "Fuck you."

"Now, that's bein' downright unfriendly, mister. Let me tell ya a little story. A day or so ago, a couple of hard-lookin' fellas in suits wandered through here. They take a boat and check out the river and all the channels, and then they leave. Now you show up."

As the first one talked, both of them had moved from the car to flank Carter. The third one, with the baseball bat, had moved around to his rear.

The second one picked up the narrative. "Now, just about a half hour ago, one o' them suits shows up again. He opens up your car here as sweet as you please, puts an envelope on the front seat, and goes down the road there like a bat outta hell. Now, my friends an' me, we'd like to know just what you're up to."

Number One chimed back in. "Yessir, we'd sure like to see what's in that envelope, and we'd like to take a look at yer wallet."

It was all clear now. Whatever this crowd was doing was against the law, and they thought Carter was the law.

In his mind he cursed Tilkoff and his KGB mentality. He had found an area for the meet that was desolate, not realizing that it could be ten times more dangerous than a crowded city where outsiders weren't noticed.

There was no way out of it. Carter didn't dare show them his identification. It had government all over it. One look and these boys would pop their corks.

"Gentlemen, whatever you're thinking, you're wrong. I swear, I'm in and out of here and . . ."

They came for him, all three at once, the one on the right the closest.

Carter caught him flush in the face with the bottle and rolled away from a roundhouse right thrown from his left. Just as Carter hit the ground the baseball bat came down across his back. He was already rolling, so when it hit it wasn't a killing blow.

He groaned in pain, but rolled over as he hit and brought both boots up between the bat wielder's legs. The connection was solid and brought forth an earsplitting shriek.

Carter made it to his feet with Number One coming on strong, his big paws opening and closing in anticipation.

One hand went for Carter's throat. It was a decoy. When the Killmaster went for the huge first, the other hand crashed into his ribs.

He knew something was broken or cracked even as he smashed back into the car with Ugly all over him. Carter nailed him two good ones in the kneecap with his right boot and brought both fists into his face.

The man staggered back and Carter pounded his pockets for his keys.

Too much time.

The one he'd hit with the bottle was back in the game, coming at him like a bull.

Carter grabbed an arm at the wrist and above the elbow. At the same time, he pivoted around, slammed his hip into the other man's gut, and bent.

The giant's momentum plus Carter's strength should have sent him plowing headfirst into the pickup in front of them.

It didn't.

The guy went nowhere.

Carter did. He went straight up, through the air, and landed, back first, on the truck bed. Before he could even get his breath he had almost three hundred pounds of beef straddling his chest.

He got his hands around Carter's throat and started squeezing. At the same time, he started banging it up and down.

Carter used his legs as a fulcrum to try and bounce him off.

No good.

The second giant just flopped down over them, pinning all of him to the ground. Through the film forming over his eyes Carter spotted the third one coming up with the baseball bat.

Swell, he thought. *Three rednecks do in fifteen minutes what the KGB couldn't accomplish in years.*

There was nothing but red in front of his eyes now, and his brain felt like the little ball on a roulette wheel just before it bounces into the hole.

He was going out and he knew it.

"Jesus, Mort, don't kill him." Woman's voice.

"The hell with him." Ugly's voice.

"Dammit, knock it off . . ."

It was the woman's voice again, but Carter didn't hear the end of what she said.

He started to come awake slowly, and then more rapidly when the blur in front of him became a gray-bearded face with glasses and tobacco-stained teeth.

"He's wakin' up. Welcome back to the living, son."

"Who the hell are you?"

"Local doc. Actually I'm a vet, but bones are bones. You got a few cracked ones."

Carter ran his hands over his chest. It was swathed in tape. "What else?"

"A few contusions, possible concussion, couple of

loose teeth . . . you'll be fine. Miss Loretta said you took a bad fall."

Carter managed a smile that hurt his teeth. "Not half as bad as she's gonna take."

"Don't say that, Nick, after I carried you all the way back here after your accident!"

Her face materialized on his other side. Carter was about to raise some hell, when the doctor snapped his bag shut and spoke. "Just put a little antiseptic on his face and that shoulder and he'll be fine in a day or so."

"I'll do that. Thanks, Doc."

The old man's face disappeared. Carter heard a door close, and then the faces of the two bearded gorillas appeared above him.

"Name's Mort."

"Name's Jake."

"No hard feelin's."

"Nah, we was just funnin' with ya a little. Sorry."

"Yeah, sorry."

"Me too," Carter said. "You satisfied now I'm not here lookin' for you?"

"Yup."

"Yup."

"Get outta here, both of ya. I'll take care of the rest of him, like the doc said."

"Sure, Loretta. Anything we can do for ya, Carter, you just let us know, ya hear?"

"I'll do that."

They left, closing the door softly behind them, and Loretta went to work with a cotton swab.

"Ow . . . ouch . . . dammit!"

"Relax, ya don't want infection, do ya?"

"I want a drink."

She shrugged, found him a bottle, and poured. She also helped him scoot up on the bed so he could drink it.

"You're a good man. It ain't everyone would tee off

on those three like you did.''

"Yeah, that's me, all guts and no brains.''

The whiskey did wonders by the time the glass was empty. He held it out for a refill and she joined him with a second glass.

"What do you do for the State Department?''

"So you did go through my wallet.''

She nodded. "That's all they wanted to do, make sure you weren't a state cop or FBI.''

"And what if I were FBI?''

Loretta shrugged. "Swamp. Feelin' better?''

"Lots.''

That brought a smile from her that Carter decided was pure leer.

"Good. Here's yer envelope.''

It had been ripped open. Carter took out the single sheet of paper. It was a detailed map with arrows pointing upriver and then off on a small tributary. There were landmarks detailed all the way so he couldn't miss the final X'ed destination.

"That's the old Shackleford place,'' Loretta commented, peering over his shoulder. "It's empty now. The old man died about a year ago. You'll need a boat to get there.''

"And you'll rent me one?''

"Sure, least we can do.''

"Tell you what, Loretta. I won't ask you what you and your friends do, and you don't ask me what I do. Deal?''

"I guess that's fair. Friends?'' She held out her right hand.

"Friends,'' Carter said, taking her hand.

The move was smooth, right down on the bed beside him as if she had oil in all her joints.

"You know what, Nick Carter?'' she purred.

"What?''

"I'm glad as hell you're not a cop. It's nice seein' a new face out here now and then."

Her arm slipped around his neck and she offered her mouth to his. It was a long kiss, deep and open and startling. During it, her body was yielding, melting to his.

He slid his arms around her shoulders, and felt her heart beat as she leaned against his body. He let his tongue travel around the rim of her ear, feeling a shiver of desire ride through her, matching his.

"I want you," she whispered.

"Right to the point, aren't you?"

"That's the way we do things down here."

Her hand moved down between his legs, and for the first time Carter realized he was naked.

"I do believe you're up to it," she chuckled, and stood.

She moved across the room and killed the overhead light. That left only the dim light from the bathroom shining through the partially open door.

On the way back to the bed she unzipped the red dress and let it work its way down over her body to puddle on the floor. She wore no bra, and in the gloom Carter saw her slip out of the white haze of her panties.

He lay back as she moved over him, straddling him. Her ripe breasts swayed provocatively and then lowered to massage his chest as their lips came together.

Their mouths opened in a kiss that drove all the pain from Carter's body.

She guided his hands to her hips and let him move her down over him.

"There," she moaned, "right there."

Then she swallowed him and her hips twisted and surged, drawing him deeper and deeper inside her.

She was a bottomless ocean of pleasure, and Carter explored it all. The waves covered both of them with desire, and then exploded into fire.

She locked her knees at his chest and undulated wildly above him. He felt a contraction and a sudden, violent throbbing as she reached the peak of her own orgasm.

Suddenly his hips lurched and wave after wave of release surged through his body. It centered and flowed upward to his chest and down to his thighs.

"Well?" she said, again settling her upper body over his.

"All is forgiven," Carter said, grinning, already feeling himself slipping into a deep sleep.

NINE

She was gone when his mental alarm clock awakened him. It was an effort to get out of the bed, but the pain ebbed by the time he had shaved and dressed.

Outside, there was almost a poised stillness about the morning, as if it were waiting to explode.

The surface of the river, walled in by high-crowned and shadowy timber, was unbroken and dark. Little feathers of mist curled off the water to hang suspended against the backdrop of the trees.

Carter paused by the car long enough to retrieve his Luger and stiletto from the false bottom of the bag. Wilhelmina, the Luger, he slid into his belt at the back. The stiletto went into a sheath on his right leg.

This done, he moved on up to the main building. White lights coming from the windows and doorway blended with the gray tones of dawn.

Loretta Ducaine, in shorts and a man's shirt, was frying eggs on the grill. She glanced up and smiled as the screen door opened. The old man was taking some spinning lures from the showcase to the left of the door.

There was another man, dressed in pressed khakis, sitting at the end of the counter, eating. He looked to be in his fifties, and Carter guessed he was the occupant of the other lighted cabin he had seen the night before. Beside him on the counter was a hat, its band decorated with hooks and lures.

He nodded good morning to Carter and went right back to his food.

"Good morning," Loretta said sweetly. "How are the ribs?"

"Mending," Carter replied, returning her smile. "Good medicine."

Her head tilted toward the old man at the case. "Roscoe is fixing you up with some gear and a boat."

"Thanks."

"Food?"

"I could use some."

By the time she had whipped up some ham and eggs and hash browns, the other man had finished and paid.

"Good luck, Jeff."

"Thanks, Loretta. See you tonight."

Carter relaxed. Evidently the other man was a local.

She brought the food, got a cup of coffee, and sat beside him. Carter spread the map out beside his plate.

"Couple of questions?"

"Sure," she said, nodding.

"Last night, the beards, Mutt and Jeff . . ."

"Mort and Jake," she chuckled.

"Yeah, Mort and Jake. They said a couple of guys had come through here in suits and done a number up the river."

"That's right."

"And last night one of those same guys put this in my car. Were they sure he was one of the earlier suits?"

"Damned sure. That's what got 'em so riled up."

He pointed to a spot on the map. "This is where I'm going. Is there a place to land downriver from here and go overland . . . like going in the back way?"

Loretta leaned close to the map, a finger tracing it in concentration. "Yeah, right here." She explained the terrain in great detail, and also explained the pitfalls of the swamp going overland. Then she took a pencil and filled out the map with roads and an extension of the waterway beyond where he was originally directed to land.

Roscoe passed around the counter carrying a small outboard motor. "You about ready?"

"Five minutes," Carter said.

The old man went out the door, and Loretta placed her hand on Carter's arm. "You'll be back tonight?"

Carter smiled. "You can count on it."

He paid and went outside. The old man was waiting for him by a boat with a 2 painted on the bow. Fishing tackle and a can of bait sat in the bottom of the boat. The motor was already attached to the stern.

"Bass be bitin' up Lake Fargo way. If ya want cat, stay to the river."

"Thanks," Carter said, and climbed into the boat.

The motor started on the first pull, and he eased away from the pier. About two hundred yards up, the river narrowed, becoming a vast network of sloughs, channels, and swampy area in heavy timber, all connected by waterways passable to outboard craft.

Carter kept the map on his knee and finally turned off the main stream into a narrow inlet, staying close to the weed beds and fallen trees. The sun was coming out full now, but the air was still cool and fresh.

For over an hour he let the little five-horse motor move him along the route on the map. It was nearly nine o'clock when he spotted the huge fallen oak Loretta had mentioned.

He cut the motor and came to rest beneath dense, overhanging foliage along the bank. No sound broke the stillness. The channel, about thirty yards wide at that point, materialized out of the timber a quarter mile behind him and disappeared around another bend just ahead.

Carter sat still for a moment, frowning at the map without actually seeing it. The dirt road that Loretta had penciled in dead-ended against the channel he was in, near the old house.

That meant Tilkoff could have come in by car.

Two men, they had said. Why two? Could someone else be defecting with Tilkoff? Hardly.

Loretta had said the shack was about a mile from the spot where he now was.

Carter tied off the boat and slipped ashore. The trees were like a thick blanket overhead and the ground was swampy. He carefully watched the ridges as she had instructed, keeping his eye peeled for any change in color.

"Stay away from the darker green," she had warned him. "It's kiwi or swamp grass. It looks solid. It isn't. Step in it and you'll be up to your ass, or worse."

Going a mile took over two miles of zigzagging. By the time he reached the dirt road, the sun was high and he was sweating. He took off the light jacket and tied the sleeves around his neck.

Without exposing himself, he moved through the trees from the channel, the full mile to the place where it met a wider, more traveled asphalt road that ran parallel to the river.

Although there were several places a car could be hidden, he found them all empty.

Finally he rechecked his bearings and struck off through the trees again for what he hoped would be the inland side of the shack.

Catfish jumped and splashed in the black-green waters of the bayou around him. Guessing that he was close now, he moved slowly and quietly through the humid mist that shrouded the moss-draped oaks and gaunt cypress trees.

Then he saw it, a grubby one-room gray shack with the shingles peeling off the roof.

Nobody was in sight. Carter moved ahead to the edge of the trees, heat clamping on the back of his neck like a giant fist. Even the insects had suddenly shut up in the stifling humidity.

There was a walk up from the river with chest-high weeds growing on both sides of it. All the windows of the house were closed with wooden shutters. A pirogue—a local canoe—rested on two sawhorses near the rear door.

Carter filled his hand with the Luger, took a deep breath, and stepped from the trees.

When nothing moved and there was no sound, he moved toward the rear of the house. He walked around the pirogue and approached the door. It was half open.

"Anybody here?"

Silence.

He moved up the steps until the barrel of the Luger nudged the door open. He moved inside with the swing of the door, and then slid quickly to one side against the wall.

He squinted, willing his eyes to adjust to the dimness. They were almost there when a figure, hands high in the air, suddenly materialized and moved toward him out of the darkness.

"I am Sergei Tilkoff. There is no need for the gun, Carter. As you can see, I am unarmed."

"Keep coming and keep your hands in the air," Carter growled, backing out into the sunlight.

The man followed. He was small-boned and dark-skinned. His black hair was too long and it glistened with oil, combed straight back from a vee where it grew low on his forehead. His lips were full and unpleasantly red. His eyes were beady and nervous, and his nostrils flared as he breathed.

"May I put my hands down now?"

"Soon. Turn around first, lean against the wall."

His blue jacket clung snugly to his sloping shoulders and sunken chest, and his trousers were tight over plump hips.

Carter patted him down and found him clean.

"Okay, drop 'em."

Carter slid the Luger back into his belt and opened his cigarette case. "Okay, Tilkoff, let's talk."

The little man was all smiles as he came up with a lighter. It flamed and Carter bent his head.

Suddenly his nostrils filled with the fumes from the flame. The cigarette fell from his lips and he felt a coldness grip his body.

The little man's image swam before his eyes. He staggered to the side, trying to get his arms to move, trying to reach the Luger.

Nothing would work. As he turned, lurching against the wall of the house, Carter could feel the paralysis flood his body.

And around the pirogue he saw them coming, a tall man in jeans and a black sweater, and a beautiful blonde.

They were both grinning at him.

The grins were the last thing Carter remembered as he fell forward into the big man's arms.

The steel legs of the cot were bolted to the floor. The

floor itself was cement, old and cracked in many places. There was a smell of age, decay, and dampness.

The walls were yellow, weeping moisture, and there were two windows, both barred. The door was thick wood, with a small, barred opening. It looked as though it had recently been repaired. The hinges were shiny new.

Carter rolled over on the cot and touched the wall. It was damp and flakes of aged paint and whitewash came away, dusting his body and the cot.

Somewhere a woman was speaking in a dry, husky voice. The language was Russian.

"No. We want no incidents. All we want are the answers . . ."

The voice faded, came back, and faded again.

Carter tried to rise. His muscles felt like rubber, or lead, depending on how much he tried to move.

A setup. It was a setup and he had walked right into it.

His head didn't ache, but he felt lethargic. He felt as if he had to have more sleep. He knew he had been gassed and then probably doped.

Slowly, his mind got more alert.

Someone walked by the door, stopped. "Major, he is awake."

Carter recognized Tilkoff's voice. He swung himself to a sitting position on the cot. He saw a face at the barred opening. Then it moved away.

"He is sitting up."

A key rasped in the opening. The door swung wide and a woman entered.

She was blurred, but slowly, through concentration, Carter got her into focus.

"Well, I'll be damned," he growled.

She was very beautiful, a big-boned, tall woman with an oval face and a silken mass of warm, honey-blond hair that fell to her shoulders. It was an alarmingly beautiful face, yet in her green eyes there was a look of indefinable cruelty.

"Good morning, Mr. Carter."

"Morning?" His voice sounded as if it belonged to a toad.

She moved closer. Now he could see her clearly, her chic swamp attire consisting of a beige safari jacket, skintight faded denim jeans, and waterproof boots.

"I am Major Anya Annamovna Chevola."

"Good for you," Carter replied.

She was leaning over him now, the gleaming curtain of her golden hair falling forward on her shoulders, framing her perfect face. Her eyes were magnificent, a vivid green-gold, large and lustrous. And ice cold.

"How do you feel?"

"Like shit."

He lunged for her throat. As casually as if she were slapping a fly, her hand came up, centered on his face, and pushed him, hard. The back of his head made a thudding sound against the cement wall and she was over him. Her knee was in his chest and her face was inches from his.

Now he saw nothing but her eyes. They were narrowed to angry slits, all at once giving her face an ugly expression.

"Listen and listen very carefully to what I have to say."

"Where am I . . . Siberia?"

"You are about ten miles from the old shack where we gassed you."

"Nice work. I actually thought Tilkoff was for real."

"He is," she replied, backing off so that Carter could get his breath. "We don't want an incident, and we don't want to start a tit-for-tat, body-for-body war between our agencies."

"That's nice of you."

"You will not be harmed. We merely want information . . . information that, in the long run, will serve both sides."

She paused, waiting for Carter to reply. When he didn't, she produced two cigarettes, lit them, and put one between his lips.

"Several years ago you helped in the defection of a woman named Nina Kovich." Again she paused. When there was no response, she continued. "The woman became Nina Cavetti. We knew her identity all the time but chose to do nothing . . . at least the First Directorate chose to do nothing. Certain men, however, decided to use her. Those men were traitors to the party."

"Good for them."

The whack across his face was like a rifle shot. It sent Carter sprawling off the cot.

"I said you wouldn't be harmed," she spat. "I didn't say you wouldn't be hurt."

To Carter's surprise, she helped him back onto the cot and lit a fresh cigarette to replace the one she had smashed.

"Comrade Tilkoff, of course, lied about his defection. It was necessary to get you away from Washington to a place where we could interrogate you quietly and privately."

"What about the part about Shalin, Gusenko, and Leventov?"

"That was true."

"And the Andropov file?" Carter asked.

"Also true . . . sad as it is."

She stood and began to pace. As she did, and talked, Carter couldn't help thinking what a waste all that beauty was on a KGB major.

"They stole the microfilm and got it out of the country. Nina Kovich's brother, Joseph Kadinskov, helped them . . ."

Then Carter remembered. It all fell into place.

"How?" he asked, already knowing.

"We're not sure. We think the files were smuggled out in a body. You helped Kadinskov and his sister escape Shalin's assassins, did you not?"

Carter decided he could go that far. "Yeah, I did, through Finland."

"We think Joseph Kadinskov knows the identity of that body. We have been looking for him for nearly a year and a half, to no avail. We must find him, Carter. That is why we staged all this."

Carter shook his head and mashed the cigarette out against the wall. "Then I'm afraid both of us are out of luck."

"What do you mean?"

"I don't know where Nina and Joseph are. I'm sure they have new identities now, and I don't know those either."

"You're lying."

"Afraid not." He went on to explain the deaths of the three agents in Finland, and how he had separated from the brother and sister.

"Where were they set up for from Finland?"

"I don't know that, either. As far as I know, they disappeared."

Any good agent is a good liar. Carter was no exception. But it is also a fact that a good agent can spot a lie.

Comrade Major Chevola was an excellent agent.

"We'll see," she murmured. "Here."

She dropped the pack of cigarettes on the cot along with a book of matches, and left.

An hour later, Sergei Tilkoff appeared with a tray of food.

"I'm not hungry."

The man shrugged. "Then don't eat."

But Carter was hungry. He devoured the food down to the last morsel of bread. Within minutes after finishing, he knew the food had been drugged—not heavily, only with a tranquilizer to keep him tame.

It was another hour before they appeared again, all three of them.

Major Chevola entered first. Her red lips were like a sneering gash on her face, and her green eyes flashed.

She had shed the safari jacket, and her full breasts filled her camp shirt to the bursting point. As she approached the cot, her breathing increased.

And she carried a cotton-wrapped hypodermic needle in her left hand.

Major Chevola pressed the stop button on the tape recorder and leaned back with a sigh.

"Enough—it should be more than enough to find Kadinskov if we move fast enough. Yevgeny . . ."

"Yes, Comrade Major?"

"Contact Rome at once that we are on the way. We will need transportation the moment we arrive. You and Pavel will come with me. Sergei?"

"Must I?" the swarthy little man asked, sweat covering his face.

"Yes, you must. The hypos are all prepared. Give him one injection every twenty-four hours."

"But it has been two days. Surely someone is looking for him by now."

"Probably," she replied. "And when they find him I want him alive, Sergei. Make sure you keep up the intravenous feeding."

"*Da*, Comrade Major."

"We will need forty-eight hours. Be sure you don't abandon him until then."

"*Da*, Comrade Major."

His voice was only a whisper behind her as Major Chevola left the old cinder-block building and walked to the car where the two other agents were already waiting.

Behind her, in the old cell, Sergei Tilkoff lifted a bottle to his lips and looked down at his charge.

Silently, he cursed Major Anya Chevola and Nick Carter alike as he drank.

Forty-eight hours.

Two days.

It would be an eternity.

TEN

In the sleepy little village of Marino di Pisa, thirty miles north of Livorno on the west coast of Italy, night had brought the cool ocean breezes. And on those breezes wafted the smell of aromatic pasta from the tops of a hundred ovens.

It was almost the dinner hour.

And in an apartment on the cliff of San Gordo above the village, Luigi Corelli set down his aperitif and achingly pulled himself from his favorite chair.

He paused long enough to rub the constant pain from his right leg. At the same time, he cursed the terrorist jackals who had caused his early retirement by shooting him. When the leg was mobile, he moved across the room to a small wooden stand beside an enormous fish tank.

This was his life now: his plump, loving wife, Rosa, and the fish he loved to watch and care for.

Carefully he prepared the food and watched them slither through the doors and windows of their underwater castles. When it was ready, he sprinkled it liberally over the water.

He chuckled contentedly as he dropped each spoonful in, taking delight in watching the fish dart about and suck the food in greedily as it filtered down through the water.

There was a buzz from the outside bell. Corelli lifted shaggy black brows in surprise and took a stubby pipe from his mouth. He was expecting no callers. Perhaps it was Rosa. She was always forgetting her key when she had to rush out to the market in the midst of preparing a meal.

Another buzz, this time louder and more insistent.

"Momento, momento."

Corelli sprinkled the last of the fish food into the tank. He wiped the crumbs on his undershirt and limped to the door. He pressed the button to release the outside catch, and pressed his ear to the door.

When he heard the click of high heels on the tiled floor, he assumed it was the pretty young woman, Adriana, from next door. She also often forgot her key.

But then he knew it wasn't Adriana. The footsteps stopped at his door. And there was a knock.

"Yes?"

There were two of them, a man and a woman.

The woman was a ravishing blonde, her hair in a tight chignon that hardened her features but agreed with the severe navy suit she wore.

The man was big, and wore a rumpled black suit, white shirt, and dark tie. His features were square and placid, as was the faint smile on his thick lips. Only the eyes weren't placid. They were blue and hot with menace, as was the silenced automatic in his right hand.

As one, they moved forward, the man curling a leg around the door, closing it.

Corelli moved back a careful step or two without saying anything. The blood was pulsing through his temples, but he took a steady drag on his pipe and let none of his inner alarm show through. He was an old-timer who had survived more than his share by reacting faster than most. Right now, his one definite reaction was that the big man looked like a fellow who liked to kill.

"Signore Luigi Corelli?" the woman asked.

"*Si*. What do you want?"

"Are you alone, Signore Corelli?"

"Yes, my wife had to run to the market."

"We want to ask you a few questions, Signore Corelli. That is all, I assure you." Her smile and her features were almost angelic when she spoke. She turned and whispered to her companion.

The big man nodded and centered the muzzle of the gun on Corelli's stomach. He did not take his eyes from Corelli's face as the woman went through the house, checking every room. At last she returned.

"He is alone. Sit down, signore."

Stay calm, Corelli thought. *Stay calm and find out what they want.*

"Who are you?"

"That is not important. Sit!"

He bobbed his balding head and shuffled across the room to an old rocking chair, his favorite.

The woman took a plastic identity card from her purse and held it up. "You have worked with this man in the past?"

Corelli glanced at the card.

"So?" He looked into the bowl of his pipe and poked a forefinger in to tamp down the hot ashes.

"A few years ago you got papers of Italian citizenship, passports, and work permits, at the request of Nick Carter, for a brother and sister who were defecting from the Soviet Union." The identity card went back into her purse and two small photos took its place in front of Corelli's face.

Corelli recognized them instantly, but he kept his face a stone mask and said nothing.

"This is the man and woman, is it not?"

"I have done what you say so many times, for so many people . . ." He shrugged as he let his words trail off.

The woman stepped aside and the man took her place. He thrust both hands into his trouser pockets and rocked back on his heels. His eyes were slitted but his face remained coolly impassive.

"We want their new names, Signore Corelli, the names on the papers you got for them. And we want their location."

Still Corelli said nothing. He rocked placidly back and forth in the old-fashioned chair, his fingers around his pipe, his hands close to his belly.

"Names," Yevgeny hissed, and hit Corelli on the back of the neck without warning.

Yevgeny was a bull of a man, his shoulders meaty and powerful under his clothing. The blow slammed Corelli to his knees on the floor.

Corelli clawed with both hands at Yevgeny's trousers, trying to rise, but the big man gripped his fingers and squeezed until the knuckles broke.

Corelli fell away with a groan of pain, and Yevgeny kicked him savagely in the ribs. Before he hit the floor the Russian hauled him back up with one hand and punched him in the mouth, again and again.

When blood and teeth spewed from the Italian's mouth to Yevgeny's satisfaction, the big man flung him sprawling across the floor.

Anya Chevola stood calmly to the side, observing. Yevgeny worked with speed, efficiency, and relish. But after another ten minutes of ruthless sadism, she knew that Corelli wasn't going to give them the information they wanted.

They couldn't use drugs as they had on Carter. It would take too much time.

She glanced calculatingly around the room, and noted one whole wall lined with tanks of fish. She moved close and watched the beautifully wrought Italian castles inside and the plump goldfish swimming lazily about.

"Yevgeny . . ."

"Da?"

"Bring him over here." The big man did as he was told, and Anya Chevola leveled her icy green eyes on him. "Signore Corelli, you are a foolish, idealistic man. Nick Carter has already told us much of what we want to know. It was he who gave us your name and the means to find you. Why don't you tell us what else we want to know?"

"I . . . I don't know anything . . . I swear," Corelli replied through bruised lips.

"Pretty fish, Signore Corelli," she said.

"They are good friends, the fish," Corelli sputtered.

Anya reached one delicate hand into the nearest tank while Luigi Corelli watched her through swelling eyes. The fish weren't afraid of the woman's gently swirling hand in the water. They were accustomed to Luigi Corelli doing the same thing each day, even moving his finger gently along their scaly sides as they swam.

"What are you doing? Don't do that!" he cried.

She cupped one fish gently in her fingers without difficulty and pulled it dripping from the tank. Then she turned so that Corelli could clearly see the flopping little fish in her hand.

"The names, Signore Corelli, and where did you resettle them?"

"You are monsters, both of you!"

Major Anya Chevola calmly put the goldfish partially in her mouth. Calmly, she bit the head off with one crush of her jaws and started chewing on it.

Luigi Corelli screamed in pain and anger. He lunged for her. Anya easily sidestepped his body and shoved him into the tank. It tipped, crashed to the floor, and fish and castles scattered everywhere.

The woman stepped forward and grabbed Corelli's hair. She dragged him easily over the slick floor to where one of the fish lay flopping on the rug. Then she pushed his face close to the floor and ground the fish to pulp under the heel of her shoe.

"This can end now, Signore Corelli, or it can continue, until all your fish are dead . . ."

"You are beasts!" he gasped, interrupting her. "They are defenseless little creatures!"

"True," she said, "But they do not *feel*, Signore Corelli. Soon your wife will be here. She will feel, Signore Corelli. I assure you, she will feel . . ."

"You have no souls . . ."

"The names, signore, and the location."

He had lost and he knew it. He couldn't fight such heartless beings. And his poor Rosa, she did not deserve this.

He told them what they wanted to know.

Anya Chevola let his head drop to the floor. She dried her hands on his shirt and turned to Yevgeny, leaning her lips close to his ear.

"Wait for the wife. Then kill them both."

Adriana Saldo ran up the stairs, her dark hair flying behind her.

It had worked. The old man, Luigi Corelli, had said

he had the clout to make it work, and it had worked!

She had gotten the government job she had coveted for so long, and she had the old man to thank for it.

Their door was open a crack, and water gushed from beneath.

Odd, she thought, of all the buildings in Marino di Pisa, they had never had plumbing problems.

She knocked and the door swung open at her touch.

Adriana started to scream, but no sound came.

Rosa was just inside the door, sprawled on her belly, the back of her head gone. Luigi was in the mess that had been the fish tanks. He was on his back and his mouth was working, gulping like one of his fish.

She continued to stand and stare, trying to scream, when she realized that there was sound coming from the old man's mouth.

Signore Corelli was still alive.

Like an automaton, the young woman walked stiff-legged across the room. She knelt and made the sign of the cross. "Oh, dear God, Signore Corelli . . ."

His eyes were open, staring, and the lips still moved. The eyes drew her down to him until her ear was nearly touching his lips.

"Stillati . . . Vito . . . Sophia . . . Stillati . . . Palermo . . . must tell . . ."

"What . . . tell what, Signore Corelli?"

Adriana lifted her head and looked down into the now sightless eyes.

She would never know what to tell. Luigi Corelli was dead.

She stood, her whole body shaking, her chest heaving with quick intakes of air.

What should she do?

Stillati, Vito, Sophia, Palermo.

My God, she thought, Sicily. Were the Corellis victims of a vendetta? Would the Stillatis come after her as

well if she told the police what the old man had said just
before dying?

She ran from the apartment, closing the door behind
her. For an hour she walked the streets of the tiny resort
village, her mind in a daze.

Finally it was fear that gripped her. She ran back to
her apartment house, but didn't enter. Instead, she
climbed in her car and drove the three miles inland to
Pisa.

She would stay with her mother for a few days and
call in sick to work.

Andriana Saldo wanted no part of it.

ELEVEN

Carter knew he was being carried. He could sense the swaying motion, and he could hear voices but he couldn't make out the words.

Every movement pained him. The pain was like a cold sword being driven through his spine until it ended just inside his skull. As it went on, he didn't care especially whether he lived or died. He merely wanted to lie still. He wanted quiet, wanted to be left to die in peace.

Then the movement stopped, and with it the pain ebbed. His body was cushioned by something soft, and he slept.

When he awakened, his head had returned to his body, but it was all floating together now. And the pain was back.

But that was good. He wasn't dead after all. You don't hurt when you're dead.

He tested one eye and got it partially open. There was a ruddy amber light all around him. The room focused . . . a chair, a woman in the chair.

The woman was familiar. She was wearing shorts, yellow shorts, as tight a fit as possible, and a green tank top that stretched like rubber over her breasts. She wasn't wearing a brassiere. She was sexy, even in sleep.

And then he remembered.

"Loretta . . ."

The woman's eyes popped open and she was instantly by his side. "Nick, thank God you're awake!"

"Water . . ."

She got him a glass of water and held it to his lips.

He went back to sleep while he was drinking it.

When he woke up again, his mind was operating better. She was beside him, sound asleep in the shorts and top. He rolled his head to the side and blew in her ear.

Her eyes opened and she rolled to her side, facing him. "You gonna live, kiddo?"

"Think so," he replied. "What time is it?"

She checked her wrist. "Five o'clock in the morning."

"What happened?"

"When you didn't come back that night or the next day, I sent Mort and Jake out to find you . . ."

"The next day?" Carter shook his head, making his brain settle in the right place, and then remembered the blond woman, the interrogation, and the hypo.

"They found the boat but no you, so they started asking up and down the river. Doesn't much get by the river people. They know every boat and car that don't belong. They found you, drugged, in the old abandoned chain gang work camp."

"Loretta, how long has it been since I left your place?"

"Four days."

Carter's eyes opened wide. "Four days? Jesus, got to get to a phone."

But it wasn't that easy. His legs were rubber. Loretta had to hold him up and walk back and forth with him across the room before they would gain some strength and the buzzing in his head would stop.

"You need some food."

"Telephone first, then food."

They were in her quarters behind the café. She managed to get him to the front and pull up a stool for him to sit on.

"I'll make some soup."

"Yeah, soup," Carter said, and dialed the Washington emergency number. The operator answered on the first ring, verified Carter's code, and patched him through to Hawk's residence.

The AXE chief's sleepy voice answered, but he became instantly alert when Carter identified himself.

"It was a setup. They wanted a rundown on Joseph Kadinskov and his sister, the ones I got out through Finland."

"After all this time?" Hawk growled. "What makes them so important now?"

Then Carter dropped the bomb. "The file Andropov kept on his cronies was for real. General Shalin and his boys got the microfilm out of the country inside a corpse. Kadinskov helped them. The main honcho is a woman, a Major Anya Chevola. From the sound of it, her job for the last three years has been to get that file, or make sure no one else gets it."

"And they think they can find it through Kadinskov?"

"Evidently," Carter said. "They used drugs on me, so I don't really know how much I told them. I couldn't have told them too much, because I don't know where the hell Joseph and Nina are myself."

"Does anybody?"

"Maybe," Carter sighed. "That's what worries me. Can you have Central get in touch with a CID man in Rome named Salvatore Mandetti, and have him call me here?"

"Give me the number."

Carter read off the number on the pay phone and hung up.

He walked slowly back to the counter where a bowl of steaming soup and several squares of warm corn bread awaited him. The food gave him new life.

"Better?"

"Much. I could use a shower and a shave."

"You'd better make it a bath, and a French one at that. The doc was here while you were out and changed your bandages. Get 'em wet and they'll never dry."

She filled the sink while Carter devoured a second bowl of soup.

"Ready."

He found her naked, standing by the sink, washcloth in hand. He arched one eyebrow.

She ran the bar of soap between her breasts.

It was one hell of a bath.

The phone rang just as Carter finished dressing. Loretta made no move to answer it, which told Carter that she was keeping to her promise of noninvolvement. Not once had she asked a single question.

"Hello?"

"Rome calling a Mr. Nick Carter."

"Speaking."

"Go ahead, sir."

"Carter, this is Salvatore Mandetti. Your office just found me."

"It's about Luigi Corelli. I want you to find him and put a couple of men on him until I can get there . . ."

"You're too late, Carter."

A chill gripped his spine and his knuckles went white

on the phone. "What do you mean, too late?"

"Corelli and his wife were murdered the day before yesterday in Marina di Pisa."

"Dammit!" Carter hissed between clenched teeth.

"We'd like some kind of statement from you, since you inquired just before—"

"I'll give you a statement, Mandetti, in Rome, just as soon as I can get there. In the meantime . . ."

Carter gave the Italian as good a description of Anya Chevola and company as he could.

"Russians?"

"That's right. It's odds on they were responsible."

"That puts it square in my lap. I'll get the locals out of it and put the word out on those descriptions. What's the motive?"

"Can't tell you that over an open line. I'm getting the first flight out. See you in Rome in the morning."

"Good enough. I'll have a driver waiting for you at the airport. *Ciao*."

Carter hung up the phone and turned. Loretta was standing in the dim light by the counter.

"You're leaving."

"Have to."

"You'll want these." She reached under the counter and came up with the Luger and the sheathed stiletto. As she handed them over, her dark eyes looked almost shyly into Carter's. "Rome's a long ways from the bayou."

Carter smiled. "Yeah, but maybe I'll come back for some real fishing."

TWELVE

It was already a hot morning, windless and still, when the plane set down at Leonardo da Vinci Airport. Carter had the front seat in the first class section and was the first one out the door when it opened. Just as he emerged, a steward passed him the sealed airline bag containing his weapons.

A tall, thin man in a dark suit met Carter at the baggage claim area.

"Signore Nick Carter?"

"*Si.*"

"I am Bartolli." They both flashed IDs. "This way, please."

The car, motor running, was in a No Parking zone. Carter tossed his bag in and followed it.

"You in on this?" Carter asked.

The other man nodded. "For the last two days."

They small-talked through Rome traffic, so by the time they hit the CID headquarters building on the outskirts of the city, Carter had a bare-bones background.

"Fourth floor—secretary's got your name."

"Grazie."

The secretary was middle-aged and looked tired. "Go right in. He's expecting you."

Carter dropped his bag by her desk and went into the inner office.

Salvatore Mandetti was small and probably dapper at most times. Now he wore a rumpled blue suit and no tie. His shirt collar was curled and dirty, and he needed a shave more than Carter did. Also, the whites of his eyes were yellowish and red-flecked, and his hand, holding a cup of coffee, trembled.

He stood when Carter entered, and they shook hands.

"You've been at it for a while," Carter said, taking a chair.

"Yes, and even heavier after I talked with you. Corelli was well liked around here."

"He was a good man. Anything yet on Chevola and the other two?"

"Nothing," the other man said, and then sighed. "But then we don't always get the cooperation between agencies we'd like. I'm sure you know about that."

Carter nodded. "Believe me, it's not just indigenous to Italy. Want to give me a rundown?"

Mandetti took a swig of cold coffee. "They were killed in their apartment. It's in Marina di Pisa, above Livorno. The place was ransacked, but as near as we could determine nothing was taken. After I talked to you, we sure as hell ruled out robbery."

"How did they get it?" Carter asked.

"Nine millimeter, no casings, so it was impossible to get a good make. The wife took two in the back of the head. Luigi got three . . . one in the gut and two in the chest."

Mandetti passed some photographs across the desk. Carter looked them over and ground his teeth.

"Jesus."

"I agree, very messy. Want to give me your end of it?"

Carter told him the whole of it, right from the beginning until the hypo in his arm.

When he fell silent, the Italian whistled and dropped his head into his hands. "Looks like we've both got a big one by the tail. Any pictures of the brother and sister?"

"None on our side. Did you pick up anything in the Corelli apartment they might have missed?"

"Nothing. And we've gone over every line of Corelli's case file. There's nothing in it that mentions your people."

Carter helped himself to a cup of coffee and regained his seat. "There wouldn't be. He did it outside the agency, as a personal favor to me. Can I see the lab and coroner's physical assessment of the bodies?"

Mandetti fingered a stack of file folders and passed two of them across the desk. He stood and got himself a fresh cup of coffee as Carter read.

The lab report turned up some alcohol in Luigi Corelli's body. Other than that, it gave Carter very little.

The coroner's on-site physical description was a lot more helpful. He read, reread, and then skimmed certain passages a third time. Carter had read a thousand such reports, and while he knew little or nothing of medicine, he had become familiar with certain terms.

He looked up. When he spoke, Mandetti swiveled around from the window.

"His fingers and wrist were broken, as well as a collarbone. Also, there were several contusions on the face and shoulders, as well as a few cracked ribs."

Mandetti nodded. "Obviously they worked him over pretty hard before they killed him. At first we figured that could mean a lot of things. After I talked to you, I figured they tried to get information from him . . ."

"Names and places," Carter said, to himself as much as to the other man. "The question was, did he tell them?" The Killmaster dropped the lab file back on the desk and paced, again reading the physical file, this time concentrating on the autopsy. "Could you get me in touch with this Dr. Petrelli?"

"Sure." Mandetti reached for the phone. It took less than a minute and he was explaining to the other end who Nick Carter was. That done, he handed the instrument to Carter.

"Hello, Doctor, this is Carter," he said in Italian.

"Yes, Signore Carter, what can I do for you?"

"In your autopsy report, you've got a thorough description of the three wounds that killed Luigi Corelli."

"Si."

"Angle of entry, depth, damage to internal organs . . . could you explain that to me in layman's terms?"

"Of course. One moment—I have a copy of the report right here on my desk. Yes, here it is."

Carter closed his eyes while the doctor translated from medicalese. By the time he got to the end, the Killmaster thought he might have something.

"Thank you, Doctor. Now, tell me, would you say that Rosa Corelli was killed instantly?"

"No doubt about it. One bullet severed her spine at the base of the brain, the other entered the brain itself. Either one would have caused instantaneous death."

"I suspected as much. Now, you stated in your report that Luigi Corelli had traces of blood and skin, not his own, under his fingernails."

"That's correct. I believe I penciled in a hypothesis on the report that Signore Corelli probably struggled with his attacker before being shot."

Carter lit a cigarette, mulling this over.

Luigi had struggled. That was why he'd been shot, three times in the front. It was a much sloppier kill than was his wife's.

"Is there anything else, Signore Carter?"

"Yes, just one more thing. Could I assume, from your analysis of the report, that none of the three slugs in Luigi Corelli was a kill shot? By that I mean, instantaneous death?"

This time there was a long pause before the doctor replied, and when he did, he seemed to be picking his words very carefully.

"I am afraid that is an imponderable. Signore Corelli could have died at once, or shortly after being shot. Or he could have lived for a certain amount of time."

"Which is it, Doctor?"

"You're putting me on the spot, Signore Carter."

"I know. There is no mention in the report about blood loss."

"There were two reasons for that. Two of the bullets hit blood reservoirs that would flow after the heart stopped beating. Also, if you look at the photographs, you will see that there were two broken fish tanks. The water from one spilled directly over the body. Because of this, it was impossible to determine the amount of blood from the exterior evidence."

"Then let me put it this way, Doctor. With the wounds that he suffered, could Luigi Corelli have lived for a period of time after he was shot?"

Another long pause. "Yes, it would have been possible."

"Thank you very much, Doctor."

Salvatore Mandetti was frowning when Carter hung up the phone. "If you're thinking about a last statement, forget it. He was very, very dead, and had been for over three hours when he was found."

"Who found him?"

"Woman in the lower apartment. Here's her statement."

Carter scanned it quickly. The woman was Teresa Genova, age seventy-one. Water seeping through her ceiling drew her to the Corelli apartment. She knocked, opened the door, and saw the bodies. Her screaming brought the old man, Guido Improta, who lived in the other downstairs apartment.

It was Improta who called the police.

"According to this," Carter said, "neither the Genova woman nor the old man entered the apartment."

"That's right."

"Got a magnifying glass?" Carter took the glass and placed it over the closeup photo of Luigi Corelli's body. "See? Here in the rug? Those are imprints of a woman's high-heeled shoes, spike heels in fact." The thick rug, drained, left both of those prints clear.

Mandetti shrugged. "Anya Chevola?"

"No way. I had a run-in with Major Chevola, a real closeup one. The major is a big woman, maybe six feet. And she was proportioned big all over, right down to her feet. I'd say these prints were made by a small woman, five feet, maybe a hundred pounds."

"Well, I'll be damned . . ."

"Mandetti, I'd like copies of all the interrogations done on people in the building, and any of the friends that could have dropped in that night. Also, a set of these pictures."

"Take those. They're copies."

"And I'd also like to go up there and look around . . . now, if possible."

"No problem. I'll get you a chopper to Pisa and have a car waiting for you there."

While Mandetti was on the phone, Carter gathered all the material in one envelope.

"You're set. Bartolli will drive you to the helipad."

"Thanks. I suppose you're going through all of Corelli's contacts and the informers he had while he was still active?"

"We're doing that now. It's taking time. He was in the agency twenty-seven years."

"I'd like a copy of that list."

"Have it for you when you get back."

"Again, thanks," the Killmaster said, and headed for the door.

"Carter . . ."

"Yeah?"

"Call me."

"I'll do that."

THIRTEEN

It was dusk and the sun was setting spectacularly over the horizon as Carter maneuvered the car down the winding road from Pisa to the marina village. The sky was slashed with strokes of flaming red and burnt orange as the sun itself became only a sliver on the horizon.

He easily found the single good hotel, and registered. In his room, he changed shirts, splashed some water on his face, and pulled on a casual windbreaker.

Back downstairs at the desk, he wrote an address on a pad and turned it around to the clerk. "Where can I find that?"

"It is up there, signore, in the San Gordo. Only one apartment house is finished completely." A shrug. "The builder ran out of money."

It was only a five-minute drive, and Carter could see what the clerk had meant. One four-unit apartment house was completed. Beside it there were two half-finished shells.

No wonder there had been no witnesses outside that night. The only residents were those in the four units, and there were no other dwellings on the cul-de-sac that overlooked the marina and the ocean.

During the chopper flight from Rome to Pisa, he had gone over all the statements and was able to eliminate the eight names of Luigi and Rosa Corelli's friends. None of them had been anywhere near the apartment that night, so there was no chance of jarring something out of them they might have missed.

He would have to concentrate on Corelli's neighbors, the names he was staring at right now on three mail boxes.

Before going to the lower door marked "1," he stepped back out of the alcove for a second.

There were bright lights on in both lower units. Dim light showed through closed drapes in one of the upper units.

He stepped back into the alcove and knocked.

The door opened and an elderly woman appeared. Her face was seamed with wrinkles, and her while hair straggled out from a few plastic combs. She wore a long, plain black dress, black stockings and shoes, the uniform of a widow, but her bright eyes were blue.

"Signora Genova?"

"Si?"

"My name is Carter, signora," he replied in careful Italian. "I am with the government. I would like to ask you a few questions about the night of the tragedy."

He flashed his credentials long enough for her to see that they were official, but not long enough to let her read them.

"Come in."

She moved back, and Carter followed her through a musty living room into a smaller, cozier sitting room with plants everywhere. Chairs were arranged around a small, homemade round table.

"Sit."

"Grazie."

He sat down. A huge, long-haired cat leaped from another chair, walked around his leg, sniffed, and hissed at him.

"Benito, come." The cat jumped into the old woman's lap, made two turns, and settled.

"Benito?" Carter asked.

"I named him after Il Duce. He is a tyrant with a terrible temper. What do you want to know?"

"What happened that night, what you saw, heard."

"I told the police."

"I know. Would you tell me again?"

With a shrug she launched into it. The story was almost verbatim to the one in the folder on his lap.

"You heard no car that night?"

"No, and I hear every car that comes up here. The young boys and girls like to come up and park on the cliff and do the things young girls and boys do. I heard your car just now."

"What about anyone on the stairs?"

"I thought I heard Adriana come home, but I was mistaken. She wasn't here that night."

"That wasn't in the report. You told the police you heard women's heels on the stairs."

"I did, but it couldn't have been Adriana. She wasn't here that night. Guido Improta pounded on her door to use her phone to call the police. She wasn't home, so he had to go down the hill to the market."

"You and the Improtas have no phone?"

"No, signore. We are poor people, retired."

"I see." Carter stood. "Thank you, Signora Genova."

She shrugged. "Make sure the door is locked when you close it."

"I will."

The cat hissed at Carter again as he left.

He used the same intro on the couple across the hall. They invited him in reluctantly, but didn't offer a chair.

Gina Improta was quiet, prim, and white-haired, with a sickly narrow face and a small, dry-lipped mouth. Guido Improta was pasty and flabby-faced, quiet and untidy. He was well past middle age, but his sparse gray hair was combed crosswise over his skull and seemed artificially waved.

While Carter questioned him, the man had a remote, faraway expression in his eyes, as if he weren't listening.

"Signore Improta, suppose you tell me in your own words what you did that night?"

It was rambling, but fairly close to the same story Carter had read in the report. While he spoke, his eyes wandered, his lips were wet, loose and purplish, and his jaw was slack.

Carter was believing only half of what he heard. Something was wrong, but he couldn't put his finger on it as he stood there, stiff, while they sat on a pillow-covered sofa.

The inside of the apartment surprised him. It had a kind of gracious dignity. There were some oil paintings on the walls, and they looked like originals. The furniture wasn't department-store cheap, either. The tables were hand-carved, burnished antiques, and there was a deep, rich Oriental carpet on the floor.

"I understand you don't have a phone, signore."

"No, no, we do not."

"You can't afford a telephone?"

"No, no we cannot."

Carter went around the room, pausing now and then to point out various objects and mention an approximation of their value.

"What did you do before you retired, Signore Improta?"

"I . . . I was with the maritime, at Genoa."

Carter smiled. That explained it. All the objects in the room were either graft payoffs or stolen outright from the docks at Genoa.

Carter bluntly said so, watched the impact his words had on the couple, and moved in for the kill. "Suppose you tell me just what you saw that night, signore," he growled.

"Get out! Get out of my house!" the man blustered.

"If I do, I'll come back. With the police."

Signore Improta broke, the words gushing from his lips like Niagara Falls. Yes, he admitted, he saw a man and a woman go up to the Corelli apartment, and he saw them leave. The description fit Anya Chevola perfectly. The description of the man also fit the giant who had stood in the shadows of Carter's cell door.

Signore Improta finished, sweating, and his wife took it right up.

"And . . . and we said we didn't go into the apartment, but I did go in . . . I just wanted to look around . . ."

"Shut up, woman!"

"No, Improta, *you* shut up!"

"Go on, signora," Carter prompted. "You went in . . ."

"Yes. They didn't like us. I just wanted to see her things . . ."

"Was Luigi Corelli still alive?"

"Oh, Lord, no. He was dead—I'm sure of it."

"Did you crouch beside the body?"

She gasped and made the sign of the cross. "Oh, no, I

would never do that! I just wanted to look at Rosa's clothes. She was always so turned out . . ."

Carter's eyes traveled down to the woman's feet. "Were you wearing those shoes that night, signora?"

She looked down at the low, worn, flat-heeled shoes. When she looked back up, her face had turned into something vile.

"Of course I was. These are the only shoes I own."

"I swear, woman, be quiet!" her husband hissed.

She snorted derisively in his direction. "Him, with all his money, wouldn't let me buy another pair of shoes."

It was mini-World War II time between them right there in the tiny living room.

Carter slipped out before it came to blows. He was about to push the buzzer beside the door guarding the stairs to the second floor, when he thought better of it.

The third key on his ring of masters opened it, and he slipped inside. Quietly, he moved up the stairs. The Corellis had lived in number 3. He knocked on the door of number 4.

The door opened a crack and a hollow, female voice came from the darkness. *"Si?"*

"My name is Carter. I'd like to talk to you about the Corelli murders." He held up his credentials case. A slender hand came through the crack and snatched it.

"You are American?"

"Yes, I am working with the Italian government. You are Adriana Saldo?"

"Yes." The case was shoved back into his hand. "I told the police and the men from Rome everything I know."

The door started to slam. Carter thrust his foot between it and the jamb.

"Signorina Saldo, I was also a good friend of Luigi Corelli."

He could sense the hesitation, and then, "All right."

He withdrew his foot. The door closed and he heard the chain drop. Then it opened again.

She was about twenty, give or take a year, and small but inclined to plumpness, with almond-shaped black eyes that darted. Her black hair hung straight past her shoulders and was pulled back from her face with a tortoise-shell band.

Carter stepped through the door and she closed it behind him. "This way."

The apartment was smaller than the ones below, with just one bedroom and bath, a tiny kitchen, and a medium-size living room with a dining area at one end.

He waited for her to seat herself in one of the two armchairs. When she did, he took a hard, upright chair, turned it around and sat astride it with his hands folded along the back.

It was a calculated move of power, and it worked. She shifted nervously in her own chair as he looked at her quietly.

Up closer and curled in the chair, she looked even younger, vulnerable and innocent. But Carter knew by bitter experience how deceptive such an appearance could be.

"Well, signore, what do you want to know?" Her voice was surprisingly low and husky for such a petite young woman; there was nothing little-girlish about it. But Carter did detect a slight tremor.

"According to the statement you gave the police, you weren't home the night of the murders."

"That's right. I was at my mother's in Pisa. I drove down that evening from work."

"You didn't come home first?"

Her nostrils flared slightly and her eyes opened a little wider. "No. My mother wasn't feeling well."

"And you took care of her for three days?"

"Yes."

"You phoned the place where you work and said *you* weren't feeling well."

"That's the only way I could get off."

"And you came back yesterday?"

"Yes."

"Not before?"

"No."

He hammered her, asking question after question and going back and asking them again.

At one point she got rattled and jerked her feet from beneath her in the chair. They hit the floor and her hands came down on the table between them.

"I told you that already! How many times must you ask me the same thing?"

Carter fell silent. He opened the envelope and extracted the photographs. As he did, he continued to study her.

She was all ovals . . . the curve of her eyebrows, the shape of her face, the fullness of her breasts with the tight blouse tied beneath them. His eyes wandered down to her feet. They were very tiny in a pair of open slippers.

"How much do you weigh, Adriana?"

"What?"

"How much do you weigh?"

"What does that have to do with—"

"How much?" His voice was like thunder in the quiet room.

Her lower lip and chin quivered and she pressed her hands harder to the table to keep them still.

Her nails were bitten close. When she became aware that Carter was looking at them, she quickly drew her fingers in, clenching her fists.

Again their eyes met.

"A hundred pounds."

"You were friendly with the Corellis?"

"Yes . . . very." Her voice grew quiet, and he could

see the tears in her eyes. "They were very nice people."

"Yes, they were. I want you to look at this picture."

She barely looked at it and flung it from her instantly, curling into a ball and breaking into heavy sobs.

Carter lit a cigarette, turned the chair around to face her, and leaned back. For a full five minutes he let her cry.

"May I use your bathroom?"

She nodded and kept sobbing.

Carter closed the door of the bedroom quietly behind him and switched on the light. Gently, he opened the door to the closet. It was a walk-in, clothes on both sides and a hanging shoe rack on the back wall.

There were several pairs of spike-heeled shoes in the pouches, and three pairs of boots on the floor with the same style heel.

All of them were size 36—in America, a size 5.

He flushed the toilet and returned to the living room.

Adriana had regained most of her composure. "Will that be all?"

"Almost. Is your mother sick often?"

"Yes, quite often."

"Adriana, I have a theory that Luigi didn't die immediately. I think he may have lived for a little while after he was shot."

She said nothing, keeping her eyes averted, staring at a large crucifix on the far wall.

"Adriana, are you telling me everything, the whole truth?"

"Yes, yes, damn you to hell! Leave me alone! What do you want with me? I wasn't even here! Leave me alone!"

Carter shrugged. He gathered the documents and photographs and returned them to the envelope. He headed toward the door, but halfway there he stopped and turned.

"Adriana . . ."

"Yes?"

"I understand you're starting a new job next month
. . . a good job with the Tuscany office of social services."

"Yes, it is what I am trained for."

"It will be a lot better than the waitress job you now
have in the hotel."

"I hope so."

"Luigi Corelli was always helping people, when he
could. Good night, Adriana."

He flipped a book of matches from the hotel into her
lap, turned, and walked out.

The address for Beatrice Saldo was in the heart of the
old city of Pisa, about a block from the Arno. The
apartment house looked as if a stab had been made at
renovation about fifty years before, and abandoned.

A screech erupted from inside before his finger lifted
from the bell. "Come in . . . come in!"

The door was unlocked. Carter entered and followed
the sound of ice in a glass.

Beatrice Saldo had probably been a stunning woman
with an eyeball-popping figure when she was young.
Now she was in her mid-fifties, a large, flabby woman
seated on a frayed sofa. She had one leg slung across the
other, a dimpled elbow resting nonchalantly on the
back, and she was downing large swallows of scotch
whiskey from a well-filled glass.

"You're not the boy from the grocery, but you'll do.
Sit down."

"My name is Carter, Signora Saldo."

She grabbed a bottle from a nearby drink trolley and
refilled the glass. Carter sat opposite her at a safe
distance.

She wore a short dress, her chubby legs bare above
short white socks and slippers. The dress was low-cut at

the bodice, and when she moved, both of her mammoth breasts almost burst free.

"Drink?"

"*Grazie, no . . .*" Slowly and carefully, so her inebriated mind could understand every word, Carter explained why he was there.

Signora Saldo smiled the inane, toothy smile of the drunk halfway through. By the time he finished, she was stone sober and like a clam.

No matter how rapidly he asked the questions, or how he reversed them to trip her up, she stuck to the story. A story, Carter was sure, Adriana had gone over a hundred times with her.

A half hour later, Carter stood up to leave. It was a lost cause and he knew it.

"My Adriana is a good girl. You leave her alone, you hear?"

"I'd like to, signora, I would really like to."

He cursed the whole deal during the drive back to Marina di Pisa. He was positive that Adriana Saldo had been in the Corelli apartment that night. In fact, it was probably she who had found the bodies. And, if that was the way it had happened, there was an outside chance that Luigi Corelli could have been alive and spoken to her.

Carter stopped in the hotel dining room and ate a quick bite, then bought a small bottle of brandy and headed for his room.

He had to go through three numbers before he found a weary Salvatore Mandetti.

The Italian wasn't surprised when Carter told him about the Improtas' lies. "Not much we can do about it. At least it confirms who we're after."

Then Carter told him about Adriana Saldo.

"Now, *there* we might do some good," Mandetti said. "I think a little pressure could be applied."

"That might be the only way we can get anything," Carter replied. "Set it up first thing in the morning and call me."

"Will do."

Carter hung up and moved to the big window overlooking the ocean. Taking a long sip of the brandy, he felt it burn as it went down. But the jolt cleared his mind.

He could imagine Nina and Joseph somewhere out there, running. If they were still alive to run.

He tried to reason out the Russian major's thinking. Was she going after the Andropov file? Or was she just making sure that anyone and everyone who had had a hand in the theft with General Shalin and the others was silenced forever?

No matter which way it went, it didn't look good for the brother and sister team, unless he and Mandetti's people found them before Major Anya Chevola and her gorilla.

Carter shuddered and refilled his glass.

Adriana groaned and rolled over in the bed, her eyes tightly shut, as if that could drive all thought from her mind. She was so tired, and yet she could not sleep. The picture of Luigi Corelli dead on the floor kept flooding her brain.

Finally she sighed and gave up. She pushed the covers back and slipped into a robe. Lighting a cigarette, she moved to the large square window that overlooked the marina. Far below she saw the ribbon of beach road, lit at this late hour only occasionally by the headlights of a passing car.

Drawing deeply on the cigarette, her eyes followed the road around the crescent of the beach to the only tall building bordering the marina, the hotel.

She shivered and looked up, away, her gaze scanning

the night sky. It was clear, the stars very bright, seemingly very close.

Another shudder rippled through her body and she drew jerkily on the cigarette. The stars had been very bright and very close that night, too.

Another shudder, stronger this time, shook Adriana's body. She brought her arms up to hug herself, and found her nails digging into the soft flesh of her upper arms.

It was still clear in her memory, every sound, every sight, and every smell of that loathsome night.

Also every word Luigi Corelli had uttered.

She mashed out the cigarette and got dressed.

Carter was just starting to undress, when there was a light rap on the door.

"Si?"

"It is Adriana Saldo."

He lost no time getting it open.

She stood like a lost waif, her eyes on the floor, her hands folded over her belly. She was dressed as she had been earlier, in blouse and jeans. Only now the blouse was tucked into the jeans rather than tied under her breasts, and she wore a windbreaker.

Also, her hair was in total disarray, as if she had just gotten out of bed.

"May I come in?"

"Of course."

He stepped aside and closed the door after she had passed him. She walked directly to the window and stood where Carter had been standing for the last hour.

"You went to see my mother."

"Yes."

"She called me."

Carter lit a cigarette before he spoke. "I don't think your mother has been sick a day in her life."

"She hasn't . . . other than the drink. I lied about that night."

"I know. Want to tell me about it?"

She did, slowly, choosing each word.

". . . I think he tried to tell me the names of his killers just before he died."

Carter tried to keep his adrenaline in check to keep her calm. "What did he say, Adriana . . . exactly?"

" 'Stillati . . . Vito . . . Sophia . . . Stillati . . . Palermo . . . must tell . . .' That was all he said, then he died."

"Believe me, Adriana, he wasn't naming his killers."

He squeezed her arm and ran for the phone.

FOURTEEN

Carter walked up the wooden steps to the narrow porch of the little house. The steps creaked slightly and the front door stood open behind a screen.

Tapping on the locked screen produced no answer. The house was quiet. He assumed one of them was at home or the door would not have been open.

He turned his back to the house and looked around. The grass was sparse in the tiny lawn, but well cared for, and there were flowering bushes all along the front of the house. A narrow walk ran along the bushes and turned at the corner of the building.

Carter decided to follow it.

The gate at the side of the house was latched but not locked. He reached over its top and let himself into the enclosed rear yard. Following the walk down the side of the building, he reached the rear corner and paused.

It was then that he saw her.

She was on her haunches, a small spade in her hand, pulverizing the earth around a bush, its flowers in brilliant bloom. She wore a large straw hat against the hot Sicilian sun. Her back was smooth and tanned, bare except for the tie of a swimsuit top. Her only other clothing was a pair of shorts made taut and revealing by her present posture.

"Signorina Stillati?"

She whirled around quickly, almost losing her balance, and squinted her eyes against the sun.

When she recognized him, she whooped, dropped the spade, and ran into his arms.

He kissed her deeply and then held her at arm's length by the shoulders.

"Nina, we have to talk."

It was in the set of his jaw, his eyes, and the tone of his voice.

"They have found us."

"Maybe. I'm not sure."

"Let's go into the house."

It was dark and cool inside, a welcome contrast to the blazing heat of the sun. They entered through a service porch and then the kitchen.

She removed the broad-brimmed hat and unconsciously patted her hair. Then she sat at a table, facing him.

"Tell me," she said, catching her lower lip between her teeth.

"I will. But first, where is Joseph?"

"He has a little trucking business in Trapani. He hauls fish every morning into the mountain villages."

"When does he usually get back here?"

She glanced at a small clock on the wall. "He should be here in a couple of hours . . . not much more."

"Too long," Carter said. "Do you know the route he takes?"

"Yes."

"Change clothes. I have a car at the bottom of the hill. We've got to find him."

"Tell me, Nick."

"I will, while we're moving."

Joseph Kadinskov forced the old truck up the last incline out of the village and pulled to the side.

Before him was the tortuous, snakelike road that led back down to Trapani. He had only one delivery left, the Dozi villa. A young English couple had rented it for the summer.

Normally, Kadinskov wouldn't take this terrible back road on his return trip for just one box of fish. But the English couple paid well, almost double, and they were young and in love. And he only had to make the stop three times a week, Monday, Wednesday, and Friday.

The road demanded all the power of the little truck to climb it, and then all the stamina of the brakes to hold it back going down.

Up there the breeze had stiffened to a wind, and the sun had hazed over, though it was still hot.

He lit a cigarette and eased out the clutch. Slowly he let the truck roll forward, and began to maneuver the spiral and hairpin turns of the downward road.

Now and then over the trees he could see the rest of the island and the ocean in the distance. It was a beautiful sight, never ceasing to impress him.

And then he braked hard and swung the truck between open, wrought-iron gates. He halted it in the middle of a cobbled courtyard from which wide terraced levels stepped up to a dazzlingly white stone house.

Kadinskov loved this villa. Perhaps one day he and Nina could live in such a house. When there was no more fear, when they could come out of hiding, then they could spend some of the money they had saved, and live like something other than peasants.

There was an ornate brass knocker attached to the front door, but he hardly ever had to use it. The young wife, Sabrina, always met him before he reached the door.

He was about to knock, when the door swung inward. Kadinskov narrowed his eyes. The inside was as dark as night in contrast with the glare outside.

"Signora Sabrina . . ."

Then he saw her. This wasn't the diminutive British housewife with the soft brown hair. This woman was tall, very tall, inches taller than he was, so he had to look up at her. And she had striking blond hair, pulled severely back from her face.

She motioned him inside. Kadinskov shrugged and stepped into the long hall.

"I have brought the fish," he said in the only slightly accented Italian he was so proud of.

Too late, Kadinskov saw the huge bulk of a man come out of the doorway to his left. A fist like steel hit the side of his head, knocking him to his knees.

Suddenly his arm was twisted up behind him, forcing his head and shoulders down. Kadinskov cried out as a knee crashed into his face. His arm was released, and as he fell he tried to crawl forward to escape the pain.

"Be careful, Yevgeny, keep him awake. Tilkoff, help him."

It was the woman's voice. *Yevgeny*. Dear God, they had found him at last!

Suddenly there was another man, holding his arms to the floor high above his head, and the giant was over him with a knife.

His shirt was ripped open and the big man was sprawling across his legs so he couldn't move.

Then the knife came down and he felt the pain as the sharp blade began to shave the skin from his body.

Kadinskov tried to scream, but no sound came.

"Enough, Yevgeny, for the moment."

It was the woman's voice, and now her face was directly above his. She was smiling, a leering smile.

"Go back in time, Joseph Kadinskov. There is a great deal we want to know."

It was the last village on his route. There were two small restaurants. While Nina checked them, Carter scoured around until he found the only phone.

He thought he had it now, not all of it, but enough. On the drive up the mountains between checking delivery stops, Nina told Carter every detail of what her brother had told her over the years.

Some of it Carter remembered himself, but there were a few details Kadinskov had not mentioned that night in Finland.

"Yes, she was definitely Spanish and the body was going to Madrid . . . and there was a medallion around her neck . . . a school or church. It had an engraving on it . . . we eventually translated it. It was from Our Lady of Sorrows, in Cordona."

It took three tries and a lot of screaming before he could get through to Mandetti in Rome.

"You found them?"

"I found the woman," Carter replied. "We're looking for her brother now. Listen carefully. I want you to go through Washington to Madrid . . . the very highest authority."

"I understand."

"There was a woman, young, twenty-two, maybe twenty-three. She was Spanish, and worked for a Spanish company or maybe the government in Moscow. She died in an auto accident, possibly suicide, on or about February eighth, nineteen eighty-four. Her body would have been returned to Spain shortly after that. Her home village was Cordona."

"Okay, got it all. What do you need?"

"A name, Salvatore, I need a name. I'll contact you as soon as I can get back to Palermo and the chopper."

He hung up and headed back for the car.

Carter knew that his first duty, now that he had the key, was to get to Spain. But he couldn't stop now and leave Nina alone, not until they found her brother.

She was waiting by the car.

"He was here about two and a half hours ago." She shrugged. "This was his last stop, so he is probably headed back to the house."

"All right. Hop in, let's go!"

Yevgeny emerged from the house using a towel to wipe the blood from his hands.

"He is dead."

"Anything further?" Anya Chevola asked, flipping away her cigarette.

"Nothing."

"No matter. We have enough. Get in!"

"The English couple?"

"Leave them. They know nothing that can harm us."

Yevgeny got in the car. Tilkoff started the engine, and roared out of the courtyard and down the twisting road.

They were halfway out of the mountains when Nina suddenly cried out, "Wait!"

Carter slammed on the brakes and pulled the car as far off the narrow road as he could. "What is it?"

"This is Wednesday, isn't it?"

"Yes."

"Go back to that big Y in the road. On Monday, Wednesday, and Friday, Joseph makes a special delivery to a young English couple who lease the Dozi villa."

Carter had to maneuver back and forth several times to get the car turned. Then it was a full five minutes back to the fork. He turned off onto the high road, and about a mile later Nina pointed.

"There, through those big gates."

Carter turned and rolled down the drive into a large, cobbled courtyard.

"Is that Joseph's truck?"

"Yes," she replied with a sigh.

The Killmaster slipped from the car. Just as Nina was emerging from the passenger side, he heard a sound, a pounding from above. He looked up to see a man with a gag in his mouth banging his head against a windowpane.

Instantly, Carter filled his hand with the Luger and pushed Nina back into the car. "Stay here and stay down!"

He slammed the door and took off at a run across the courtyard. The front door was ajar. He hit it and rolled, coming up in a shooting crouch at the foot of a sweeping stairway.

There wasn't a sound on the first floor. The only sound in the house was the steady pounding coming from above.

Cautiously, he went up the stairs to the second-floor hallway. There were three doors on his right, two on the left, all closed.

He guessed the last door on his right near the front of the house, and glided forward, keeping his back to the wall.

The door was locked, and he wasn't going to take the time to use one of his master keys.

Carter stepped back and aimed a solid kick. It took three before the lock gave and the door flew open.

Immediately, he assessed the situation. The wife was bound and gagged, lying on a bed. She was out cold and the side of her face was turning a nasty blue.

The husband was similarly hog-tied by the wrists and

ankles, and also gagged. From the look of his face he had taken a bit of a beating before they'd finally subdued him.

Right now his eyes were wild with fear and focused on Carter's gun.

"It's okay," the Killmaster said in English, slipping the Luger into its shoulder rig, "I'm a friendly."

He tensed his right forearm and the stiletto slid into his hand. In seconds he had cut away the man's gag and the cord binding his arms and legs.

"Oh, my God, it was frightful . . . just frightful!"

If nothing else, the educated British accent told Carter who he was. Before Carter could speak, the man bolted for his wife.

"Sabrina . . ."

Carter quickly cut her bonds and gag as her husband checked her pulse and face.

"Thank God, she's all right."

"What happened . . . quick," Carter growled.

"Three of them, a woman and two men. They came early this morning wanting to use the phone. They said they were lost . . ."

"That truck outside . . ."

"Oh, yes, Vito—he's the fish man. I heard him arrive, and then there were terrible screams. It sounded as if they were torturing the poor chap—"

Carter cut him off. "Where, what room?"

"The sitting room in the rear, I believe . . ."

He said more, but Carter didn't hear it. He was already bolting for the stairs.

One look and he knew it was all over for Joseph Kadinskov. And the poor devil hadn't gone easy.

Behind him in the hall Carter heard the click of heels. He leaped for the windows and ripped one of a pair of drapes from its rod. He scarcely had the body covered by the time Nina appeared in the door.

"Nick, what is it? What happened?"

He moved toward her, shielding the gruesome lump on the floor from her eyes with his body. But at the last second she slipped aside.

"No . . . no . . ."

"I'm afraid so, Nina. It's Joseph."

Her mouth opened to scream but no sound emerged. Suddenly she lurched forward. Carter caught her just before she reached the body.

Then she did scream, and struggled to break free.

"No, he's not . . ."

"He is, Nina. They killed him."

Then the shock hit and the scream turned into hysterical laughter.

Carter had seen it happen before, shock becoming futility.

She stood there and laughed. At first her stomach moved, rolled, then she gasped. Her laughter rang in the room, coarse, loud, and she staggered from it.

It was wild, hysterical laughter, and it cut into Carter's guts.

"Nina . . ."

She looked up at him and her eyes filled with tears. Her mouth gaped like a raw wound and her body shuddered.

"Oh, God, God, God," she whispered, unable to speak aloud.

"Nina, please . . ."

"Let me go!"

He did, and she lurched to a large, leather-covered easy chair and sank into it. She sobbed convulsively then, her shoulders shaking, eyes streaming.

Carter heard a sound and turned. It was the husband. He stood in the doorway, his eyes on the draped mound on the floor.

"Signore Stillati . . . ?"

"Yes," Carter said.

"I'm a doctor. Is there anything I can do?"

"Not for him," Carter said tersely. "This is his sister, Sophia. Can you give her something?"

"Of course."

He disappeared and was back in no time with a hypodermic. Nina was still sobbing but she was docile.

"Is your wife all right?"

"Shaken up, bruised," the man replied, sliding the needle into Nina's arm, "but she'll be all right. What in God's name is this all about? Some sort of vendetta?"

"You could say that," Carter answered. "Do you have a phone?"

"Across the hall, on the wall in the kitchen."

Carter found it and dialed the hot-line number Mandetti had given him for Palermo CID.

It was picked up on the first ring. He identified himself and quickly relayed the information, giving the location of the villa. He also identified the killers and gave the approximate time they had for a head start.

He was fairly sure they had had a plane or a fast boat ready to ferry them to a safe place in North Africa, but it was worth a try.

When he was assured that there would be a team at the villa in no time, he hung up.

Back in the other room, the wife had arrived. She sat with Nina, cradling the woman in her arms. Her husband was just sliding the drape back over Joseph's body.

Carter crouched beside him.

"Christ, they butchered him!"

"I know," Carter nodded, flipping his credentials case open. "The authorities will be here very soon. I've got to move, fast. Will you and your wife take care of her until they arrive?"

"Of course."

Carter stood and moved to the two women.

"Why?" the wife asked, her arms still around Nina, rocking her.

"You really don't want to know." He took Nina's face in his hand and tilted it up. Her eyes were already becoming glassy from the injection. "Nina? Nina, it's me, Nick."

She stared in silence.

"Nina, can you hear me? Do you understand?"

Slowly the eyes began to focus slightly. "Yes," she whispered.

"I'm going after them, Nina. You'll be all right."

He didn't know whether she understood or not.

She just stared.

Carter could feel her eyes boring into him as he walked out of the room.

Now the Andropov file took second place to the woman and two men.

FIFTEEN

Carter got directions at San Pedro del Arroyo and left the main highway. In no time the road along the Rio Adaja became little more than a dirt track.

The land was harsh, mostly barren, and became more so the higher he climbed. A huge, nearly white full moon bathed the hills in an eerie glow.

He had moved fast, flying into Madrid and jumping right into the waiting car. Hopefully he had moved faster than they had, because he could move openly.

And then he saw the sign. It was four kilometers to Cordona, about two and a half miles. His headlights told him it was straight up.

The road was merely a dusty cart path now, with a wall of rock to his right and a sheer drop-off to his left.

Far below, he heard the waters of Rio Adaja rushing down the mountain.

Suddenly he reached the apex of the road and started down. Another few hundred yards and he slowed. He could see the lights of the village and, as he drew nearer, the buildings.

There was the usual plaza, with shops and a bar-cum-café or two. Low houses fanned out from the plaza up the opposite side of the mountain.

A gas station and garage was just ahead. It was the first building before entering the village proper.

Carter pulled in.

"Señor?"

"Gasolina, por favor."

"Sí."

The attendant moved around the car to the pumps, and Carter followed. He leaned against the fender while the man pumped the gas, and stared off at the village.

White, pink, and blue houses were jammed together on each side of narrow, centuries-old dirt streets. Each of them led into the small plaza. The plaza itself was dominated on one side by the cathedral.

"Por favor, señor . . ."

"Sí?"

"The cathedral on the plaza. Would that be Our Lady of Sorrows?"

"No, señor. Our Lady of Sorrows is the convent, up there."

Carter followed the man's pointing finger. High atop the mountain he could see the imposing, rectangular shape of a large building. A tall cross on its roof stood out starkly against the sky.

"How can I get up there?"

The man chuckled, replacing the gas cap. "Walk, señor, up many steps from the plaza."

Carter gave him a large bill and he moved toward the

station to make change. The Killmaster followed and leaned over the grease-smeared counter.

When the man counted out his change, Carter reached forward and pushed it back to him.

"Tell me, has anyone else, a stranger, asked about the convent tonight?"

"No."

Carter added yet another bill from the roll in his pocket.

"Have you seen or sold gas to any other strangers tonight?"

"Our village is small, out of the way, señor. We get few tourists here."

"A blond woman, tall, very beautiful, and two men, one big, bigger than myself, the other short, pear-shaped."

"No, señor, no one like that. I would remember."

"I have something for a family in your village, something of value."

"A name, señor?"

"The family Galadin."

"*Ah, sí, sí,*" he said, nodding. "Señora Galadin lives in the small white house just before the gate of Our Lady of Sorrows. It is on your right as you climb."

"*Muchas gracias.*" Carter headed for the door.

"Señor . . ."

He turned. The man was grinning broadly.

"Yes?"

"If your friends do come this way, should I tell them where to find you?"

Carter returned to the counter, and this time peeled off several bills. "I would rather you didn't. I want to surprise them *Entiende?*"

"*Sí.* I understand, señor."

Carter drove on into the village. He found a tiny street just off the plaza where several cars were parked, two wheels pulled up onto the narrow sidewalk, their fenders nudging the buildings.

He checked the magazine in Wilhelmina, put two spare clips in his pocket, and slipped a powerful flashlight into his belt.

With the car locked, he angled back into the plaza and walked around it until he spotted the stone steps leading upward.

It was a long climb. Halfway up, he paused and lit a cigarette. From where he was, he could see all of the village, the gas station, and the road he had gone over. He could also see the same road exit the other end of the village.

He climbed again until he reached the end of the houses. The small white one at the end to his right was dark.

Carter decided to take a chance. He opened the whitewashed gate and moved up the stone walk. He rapped lightly on the door, and then again when there was no answer.

"What do you want, señor?"

Carter whirled.

He was big, about Carter's size, with narrow hips and beefy shoulders. A blue workshirt was rolled up tight over thick biceps, one of which twitched as his fingers drummed the hilt of a knife at his belt.

"I would like to talk to Señor and Señora Galadin."

The big man stepped forward a little, and Carter could see his face. It was a rugged, handsome, square-jawed face, with a sensitive mouth under a thick mustache. Carter guessed him to be somewhere in his mid-twenties. The eyes were fierce, but full of intelligence.

"There is no Señor Galadin. The old man died about a year ago."

"Then I would like to speak with Señora Galadin."

"The señora is at her evening prayers. What do you want?"

The man's black eyes hadn't left Carter's for an instant. He could almost feel the mistrust, or worse, radiating from them.

"It is a private matter," Carter said, and started to move around the man.

Suddenly a hand gripped his arm. It was like a vise, and Carter had no doubt that if he tried to break away he might get a knife in his ribs.

"Señora Galadin is an old woman, very sad. Why would you, a stranger, come to our village to see her?"

"I want no trouble."

"I take care of the old woman. You can tell me."

"I have to give her something," Carter said, gently sliding his left hand up to his lapel.

Before the other man could move or draw his knife, the snout of the Luger was under his chin.

"I told you, friend, I want no trouble," Carter growled. "But I can handle it if it comes. Try and pull that knife and I'll take off one of your ears."

Slowly the hand dropped from Carter's arm and the other one moved away from the knife.

The black eyes gleamed. "I think you should leave our village, señor. Otherwise, you might not see the dawn."

"I want to speak with Señora Galadin about her daughter. Now, tell me where she is."

"Angelina?"

"Yes."

"What of Angelina?" The voice was strangely low, husky.

"You don't hear very well, friend."

"Señora Galadin is in the chapel of the convent. She spends hours there each evening."

"Gracias." Carter backed off. "Believe me, I mean her no harm."

The Killmaster left him standing there, and walked on up the hill to the gates. They were old, rusted, and they yawned open.

He made his way through the gardens, livid with color in the moonlight, to a pair of massive oak doors with discolored bronze hinges.

Gently, Carter opened one of the doors and slipped inside. His rubber-soled shoes made barely a sound as he stepped across the stone floor and stood in the shadow of a pillar.

She was a hunched figure in the first pew. Dressed all in black in the dim church, she could scarcely be seen.

Carter could barely hear her whispering voice as she prayed.

He stood watching her for several minutes. Then, when she stood and approached the altar, he moved back to the door. When he saw her light a candle and kneel one last time, he slipped out the door.

She emerged a moment later, and Carter fell in step beside her as she walked toward the gates.

"Señora Galadin . . . ?"

Silence, not even a glance.

"Señora Galadin, I am an American. I would like to talk to you about your daughter, Angelina."

The woman stopped. Slowly she turned her sad, wrinkled face and glazed eyes up to him.

"My daughter is dead."

"Yes, I know, señora. That is what I want to talk to you about."

"My son Jesus is dead. My daughter Angelina is dead, and my husband Roderigo is dead."

She lowered her head and moved off. Carter caught up to her.

"Señora, if I could talk to you, I might be able to ease your grief."

"Go away."

"But, señora . . ."

"Go away."

Carter stopped. It was useless and he knew it. The woman was a shell. Nothing he could say would make her listen.

He lit a cigarette and looked out over the village and the roads leading into it.

When would they come? It would probably be in daylight. They wouldn't want to attract any attention while they located the grave.

Did they know that he, Carter, knew everything they did?

Maybe. Maybe not.

Either way, they would take the chance. The reward was too great.

He crushed the cigarette underfoot and struck off through the gardens around the huge old convent.

The cemetery was in the rear on a lower level. It was surrounded by a low stone wall and, even in the moonlight, he could see that it was well cared for.

He took out the flashlight and adjusted the shaded lens down to a pinpoint.

It was a small village, consequently a small cemetery, with each family plot clearly defined. Nevertheless, it took nearly an hour to find the Galadin plot.

There was one large, black marble stone. Across the top of it, in large beveled letters, Carter read: GALADIN.

Underneath to the left and evenly spaced were two names and the dates: Roderigo, Father: 1922-1985.

And just to the right: Jesus, Beloved Son: 1950-1972.

Carter measured the remaining space on the right with his fingers. There was space for two more names, but the marble was blank.

"Did you find what you were looking for, señor?"

Carter whirled with the light, coming up out of his

crouch. He was moving his right hand toward the Luger, when the shaft of light fell across the shotgun.

It was the same tall young man. Only now he wasn't alone. There were three others. They all had guns, and they were all as stony-faced and dark-eyed as the first one.

Carter moved his hands to the side. The three surrounded him instantly. They took the Luger, his wallet, and his credential case. Eventually, patting him down, they found the stiletto.

"I'm looking for the grave of Angelina Galadin. She is not buried here with her father and brother."

"You are an American?"

"Yes," Carter replied, watching the tall man scrutinize his credentials with the flashlight.

"Why do you come here looking for the grave of Angelina Galadin?"

Carter looked at the four suspicious faces, and returned to their leader.

"Who is asking?"

"My name is Luís Estabel. Angelina was to have been my bride."

The air was heavy with the scent of cigars, musky Spanish cigarettes, and beer. Somewhere in the rear a youth strummed a guitar. The café owner, a plumpish woman with laughing eyes, held court behind the bar.

The three friends, minus their guns now, sat on stools at the bar. Now and then they glanced at the table in the corner where Luís Estabel and Carter sat in shadow.

"So, you, too, feel that Angelina's death could not have been a suicide?"

"I'm sure of it," Carter replied. "I think the Russians involved had her killed because they needed a body, a foreigner's body, that could be shipped out of the country."

Estabel winced and lowered his face into his hands.

Carter remained silent, sipping his beer and waiting. When the face came back up, the eyes were alive with fury. And the face had changed color. Now an angry thread of crimson had crept under the olive skin.

"And they defiled her body?"

"Yes, but that is no matter now, Luís. The important thing is that they want to do it again. They want to come here and do it *again*."

The young man's brow furrowed, his expression one of pain, anger, and disbelief. "They would dig her up to regain this file they want so badly?"

Carter nodded. "Yes, they would." Here the Killmaster leaned forward and placed his hand on the younger man's shoulder. "If we let them."

"What can we do?"

"No, Luís, it's what *I* can do. But I could use the help of you and a few of your friends."

"Anything you want, it is yours. Tell me."

Carter lit a cigarette and slowly told the other man exactly what help he would need. When he finished, Estabel stood and walked to his friends. He exchanged only a few words, and all three of them scattered. Estabel returned to Carter at the table.

"The roads into the village will be watched every minute from now on."

"Good."

A stout woman, all in black with a bright bloom on her cheeks and alive, piercing eyes under a head of shining white hair, entered the café. She paused for only a moment and came to their table.

"This is my aunt," Estabel explained, rising until the woman was seated. "Her name is Inez. She will help us."

Carter leaned toward her. "Señora," he said, "I want you, tonight, to move Señora Galadin into your home. Will you do that?"

"I will do whatever my nephew asks of me."

"Excellent. I want *you* to move into Señora Galadin's house. Some time tomorrow, some people will come asking for the location of your daughter's grave . . ."

Carter told her, in detail, how to act and what to say. When he was finished, she rose and left without a word.

Carter turned to Estabel. "Now, Luis, tell me. Where is Angelina buried?"

"In a small plot on mountain land I own above my house. It is not far from the village. I will take you there."

They walked out of the village and up into the hills. Estabel's house had two stories and was painted stark white.

He spoke as they passed it. "I built it for Angelina and myself to live in. I live there myself now, with my sister."

It was another mile into the hills, and then they came to a grassy slope. The plot was small but well tended and alive with flowers. The marker was large, black granite.

The moment they arrived, Estabel fell to one knee and crossed himself. Over his shoulder, Carter read:

ANGELINA
BELOVED OF LUÍS

There were no dates.

It was all clear to Carter now. The death certificate from Moscow had listed the cause of death as suicide. Angelina Galadin could not be buried in the consecrated ground of the convent cemetery. Clever bastards, thought Carter angrily. The Russians had counted on an out-of-the-way burial spot, away from the town.

Finally, Estabel stood and turned to Carter. "Well, señor, have you seen enough?"

Carter looked around the rocky hillside, back at the path they had climbed, and nodded.

"It's perfect."

"Señor, you have set out this elaborate plan. I have gotten the others to help. I have agreed to never tell another person in the world what you have told me. Now, tell me the end of this elaborate scheme of yours."

"I would think, Luís, that you would have figured that out by now. I'm going to kill them. All three of them."

SIXTEEN

It was nearly eight o'clock. Already the sun was high and the small room, high in the convent, was hot.

It was a tiny room, not much larger than a walk-in closet. A narrow bed took up most of the space. Until an hour before, one of the nuns had been sleeping in the bed.

She had left quietly, without question, when she was asked.

It was a small village, the people tightly knit. Those who didn't know what the tall, dark American was doing in their village didn't ask.

The American was under the protection of Luís Estabel.

Carter stood at the open window, a pair of powerful binoculars to his eyes. Estabel was beside him, smoking, staring off into the distance.

"This woman, Nina. What will become of her now?" Estabel asked.

"I don't know," Carter replied. "She was very close to her brother. And the way he died . . ." He let the last few words trail off.

"These are very bad people who would do such a thing to Angelina and to Nina's brother. You will tell this Nina some day that her brother's death is avenged?"

It was the tone in the man's voice that made Carter drop the glasses and turn to stare. Estabel didn't look over. He just continued to stare down at the village.

"Maybe you should tell her," Carter said.

Estabel smiled. "Perhaps."

For another half hour they stood silently, and then they saw the car. It was a green Fiat sedan. When it pulled into the gas station and the woman got out, Carter had no doubts. Even from that distance her size and the sun glinting off the blond hair identified her.

"It's her," he growled.

"You are sure?"

"Positive."

"But where are the two men?"

"My guess is that they are in a café in the last village down the road. She'll probably find the grave and then go back and get them."

Estabel shook his head. "You are a very smart man, Señor Nick. It is just as you said. I will send Manuel."

Carter heard his retreat down the stairs as he watched the woman get back into the car. Just as she hit the plaza, a youth on a motorcycle roared past her down the road.

The car stopped at the foot of the stone steps in the plaza, and the woman got out. She opened the rear door and filled her arms with flowers.

Carter felt a chill as she got far enough up the stairs for him to see her face clearly.

Anya Chevola, beautiful in a tailored white linen summer dress.

He felt like a puppet master pulling her strings as she moved through the gardens and then out of sight.

By the time Carter was down the hall and at a rear window, she was in the cemetery. In daylight, it took her only a few minutes to locate the Galadin family plot.

As she knelt and ran her hand over the stone, Carter could read her thoughts from the way her face changed.

He knew when she had figured it out. She grabbed the flowers and headed for the front of the convent. She was halfway to the gate when Estabel came through it, carrying a rake over his shoulder.

Carter could almost read their lips.

"Por favor, señor . . ."

"Si?"

"I have come to visit the grave of an old friend, but I cannot seem to find it. Could you tell me where in the village the Galadin family lives?"

"*Si, señorita.* The Señora Galadin lives right there, in that white house."

"Gracias."

She almost ran through the gate and down the few steps. Inez answered her knock at once.

They spoke, and then the Spanish woman stepped out into the yard and pointed.

Anya Chevola nodded her thanks and hurried back to her car. She was through the village in no time and climbing up the tiny road that led to Estabel's home. She drove past the lane and on into the hills.

Immediately, Carter knew her intent. She would navigate around the tiny roads up there where she, the car, and, much later, her two comrades could park undisturbed later that night.

Carter barely heard Luís Estabel's tread on the stairs and then coming down the hall behind him. A few seconds later he appeared at Carter's side.

The man moved like a cat.

"Where is she?"

"Around the other side of the mountain," Carter answered.

"Scouting?"

Carter nodded, keeping the glasses to his eyes. "She'll find a good place to stash the car, and then look for a trail up the mountain to the grave without being seen from the village."

"Manuel rode back to the village of San Lierdo on his motorcycle."

"I know. I saw him leave and pass her on the road. Look . . . there she is."

For just an instant she was a white flash against the sky, the flowers a blaze of color against her dress.

"She will be at the grave now," Estabel said tightly.

"Is there any road up there they could use to get out, in case I miss one of them?"

"No, not by car. By car they would have to come back through the village. From there, if they didn't come back through the village, they would have to walk over the mountains."

"There she is again," Carter growled, "going back to the car."

"The river is about a hundred yards on that side. They could go that way, if they had a boat waiting."

"Any chance of that?" Carter asked.

Estabel shrugged. "A chance, yes, but slim."

"Have one of your friends check it out anyway."

"I will do that."

They both fell silent, smoking, waiting, watching.

It was nearly a half hour before they saw the car round the side of the mountain and head back down. Fifteen minutes later, she was through the village and gone down the road to San Lierdo.

"That's it!" Carter said. "Let's go!"

Together they descended and walked through the

gardens to the gates. They passed three sisters of the convent. The women neither spoke nor looked at them.

At the house of Señora Galadin, they stopped and knocked. The door was opened at once by Inez, and they slipped inside.

Without waiting to be asked, the woman spoke. "It was as you said. She wondered why Angelina's name was not on the tombstone in the convent cemetery."

"And you told her?"

"Yes," the woman nodded, smiling for the first time since Carter had met her. "I told her with tears in my eyes."

Estabel kissed her on both cheeks. "You should be in the cinema, Tia Inez. She went right to the grave on the mountain."

"What excuse did she give you, Señora Inez," Carter asked, "for wanting to visit the grave?"

"She said that she had been a close friend of Angelina's in Moscow, and since she was visiting in Spain, she wanted to come to Cordona and pay her respects."

Inez puckered her lips, spit in her palm, and rubbed it on her hip.

"My sentiments exactly," Carter growled. "Estabel, let's climb the hill!"

For the next half hour they walked the mountain above and below the grave. Estabel had already found the place where Anya Chevola would park the car. Carter had located a niche of high rocks where he could conceal himself yet still see them at the grave and see the car.

"This will be perfect."

They moved down the trail to the grave. The flowers Anya had been carrying now rested on the mound at the foot of the headstone.

"Bitch," Estabel hissed, and reached for them.

"No," Carter said, grabbing his arm. "Leave them."

The other man sighed. "Of course. I am sorry."

Carter turned and pointed back toward the village. "Have your friends in two trucks, one on each road out of the village. Tell them to use the flash signal when the car has passed through."

"I will."

Estabel lit a cigarette and stared at the ground in deep concentration. Carter did the same. The other man obviously had something important to say, and Carter knew he would say it when he had thought it out.

"Señor Nick . . ."

"Yes?"

"I am like a cat in the night . . ."

"No," Carter said.

"There are three of them and only one of you . . ."

"No, my friend," Carter said, resting his hand on the other man's shoulder. "I must do this alone. Believe me, blood on my hands means nothing. You, and your friends, must do nothing and say nothing. What you do not know you cannot answer for."

At last Estabel shrugged. "Very well."

"Now I must find a gully, deep, where I can bury them. The river will take care of the car."

Suddenly, Estabel turned and faced Carter squarely, a wide grin on his face, his eyes alive with a new light.

"That will not be necessary . . . finding a grave."

"What do you mean?"

The Spaniard turned back to the mound at their feet. He dropped into a crouch and let his hand move in the air over the grave.

"Why look for a grave, when one is ready-made?"

Carter blinked. "Good God, you mean you would—"

Estabel interrupted him. "All you have to do, Señor Nick, is let them dig the grave deep enough before you make your move." The dark face was smiling even more broadly when it again rolled up to face Carter.

The Killmaster spun on his heel and looked across to the next mountain and the convent of Our Lady of Sorrows.

He closed his eyes and visualized the Galadin tombstone in the cemetery. He saw his own hand stretched out, measuring the space for the names.

When he turned back, Estabel was standing, still smiling.

A slow smile crept across Carter's own lips. "You mean . . ."

A shrug, and the dark eyes flicked heavenward. "My Angelina was beautiful, and good. I do not think God considers her a lost soul. I think He is happy she rests in His hallowed ground."

A low whistle erupted from Carter's throat. "Who knows," he asked, "besides yourself?"

"Señora Galadin knows, as well as my sister, my Tia Inez, and the three you have met. They helped me move her."

"And the priest?"

"Father Penares is an old man, a very old man. He has lived his entire life in our little village. He has known us all from birth. We are like his children and can do no wrong."

"But does he know?"

"In his heart, I think he knows. And as long as the name is not on the stone . . ." Another shrug. "But now you should sleep, Señor Nick. Tonight will be a long night and you have much to do."

The two men moved down the hill and turned up the lane to Estabel's house.

It was a nice house, simple, yet an estate when compared to others in the village. It was well maintained, with a red tile roof, and the gardens surrounding it were a delightful blaze of color.

Seeing it, Carter again thought of Nina. Poor lost Nina.

She would love this house, and this peaceful little village.

"Señor Nick, one last question," Estabel asked as they entered the square, tiled entry hall.

"Yes?"

"This thing that the woman and the two men came for—it must be very valuable, very important."

"It is, to some people."

Estabel grasped Carter's arm gently, halting him at the foot of the stairs. "Tell me, Señor Nick, is it valuable to you?"

Carter did hesitate, though he really didn't need to. He had already thought out the problem and made up his mind what to do. "No, Luís, it is not important to me."

The Killmaster turned and walked up the stairs.

It would serve no real purpose, he thought. Once safely in Soviet hands, the Andropov file would soothe a lot of fears. Without it, they would always fear. In American hands, it would become merely another tool in a silent war that was already top-heavy with meaningless tools.

No, he thought, stretching out on the bed, it was better to let Angelina Galadin rest in peace.

SEVENTEEN

Carter cupped the bright tip of his cigarette and inhaled deeply. For the hundredth time since sliding down into the rocky crevice, he shifted positions to ease stiffening muscles.

A cloud cover had moved in since dusk, but it didn't smell like rain. Now and then there would be a break in the clouds and the moon would burst through for a few seconds.

Mostly it was gray, an eerie half-night light.

He checked his watch. It was nearly two in the morning. Below him, the village was completely dark. On the opposite mountain, one window was dimly lit on the second floor. Now and then from the window on the third floor, where they had stood that morning, he could see the glow of a cigarette.

That would be Estabel.

Suddenly the cigarette arced from the window and fell into the gardens. A second later Carter saw a pinpoint light from the flash, and then another.

They were coming.

Carter shifted his gaze to the road leading up from the village.

It didn't take long.

They were moving at a snail's pace in the dim glow of amber fog lights. Carter watched the lights until they disappeared. Then he followed them by the sound of their engine.

When the engine died, he moved just enough to see the trail up from the rear road. At the same time, all he had to do was swivel his head slightly and he had a complete view of the gravesite.

It was another five minutes before he saw them, all three of them, with the woman in the lead.

They were all wearing dark clothing. Anya Chevola had wrapped a dark scarf around her head to hide the glow of her honey-colored hair.

They passed within ten feet of where Carter lay concealed in the rocks, and dropped down to the level of the grave. They were clearly outlined now, and Carter could see that the two men carried shovels. The bigger one also had a pickax.

The woman spoke. "When you have it, fill the grave back in completely. Be sure there is no trace. I want it to be just as though we were never here."

"*Da*, Comrade Major."

"I will move the car back to the curve and watch the road from there. Work fast!"

"*Da*, Comrade Major."

Major Anya Chevola moved back and down the trail. Even before the sound of her footsteps died out in the night, the two men had started digging. The larger one attacked the mound with a vengeance. The short, fat one grunted from the exertion.

With every muscle in his body tense, Carter waited. Everything was ready. The silencer was securely attached to the muzzle of the Luger. The stiletto was in its chamois sheath on his right forearm, and the snap on the piano-wire garrote at his belt was loose.

Now it was only waiting.

The flowers had been carefully removed to the side. The two mounds of dirt at each end of the grave slowly grew. Eventually the men stood in the hole up to their hips. Now it was too small for both of them to work efficiently. They began to dig in shifts, the smaller man shirking, the bigger man complaining.

The woman returned.

"How much longer?"

"Two, maybe three feet, Comrade Major."

"Faster!" she hissed. "Work faster!"

"*Da*, Comrade Major."

The woman went back down the hill.

Carter began to sweat. More and more of the big man had disappeared into the hole.

He would have to move soon. The question was, which way?

Carter was about to slide backward down the rocks and go down the trail to take the woman, when the break came.

"Yevgeny . . ."

"*Da?*"

"I have to piss."

"Then piss. The time it takes will be no loss. You use a shovel like an old man dying."

The fat one whined something Carter couldn't make out, and moved off through the rocks.

Silently, Carter slithered backward from his hiding place and dropped to the soft earth between two huge rocks.

He holstered the Luger and swiftly but quietly moved

in a wide arc around the rocks until he was below the grave.

It wasn't difficult. He located the man by the sound of his stream.

And then he saw him, his head and shoulders silhouetted against the sky. Directly behind him there was an alley between the rocks. Carter moved into it, flipping the stiletto into his hand.

The crepe soles of his shoes made no sound as he moved.

Five feet . . . three feet . . . one foot . . .

The Killmaster's left arm went around the other man's throat. He jerked the head back and brought the pencil-thin blade up in a sure, violent thrust.

The blade entered dead center in the throat. It severed the windpipe and entered the brain.

There was no more than a low gurgle in the dead man's throat as he slipped to the ground.

Carter pulled the stiletto free and wiped it on the man's pants. Then he peeled off the coat and pulled it on over his own shoulders. The narrow-brimmed hat he placed on his head, and made his way silently back to the gravesite.

The one called Yevgeny was up to his shoulders now in the grave, and cursing. He barely glanced up over the rim of the hole when Carter emerged from the rocks.

"How deep do they plant them in Spain?" he growled. "I must be down at least six feet, and still nothing!"

Carter held the Luger down at his side as he moved over the open ground. He didn't bring it up until he was at the foot of the grave.

It must have been the second sight, the pure instinct of the trained agent, that made Yevgeny look up at the last instant.

He made no sound but swung the shovel in an arcing blow at Carter's middle.

The Killmaster kicked the shovel to the side with his left foot and shot the man square in the face.

The big man's arms went wide with shock and he fell back into the grave.

But Carter didn't stop.

He dropped to one knee, leveled the Luger on the man's chest, and emptied the clip.

"For Joseph, you son of a bitch," he whispered.

When the hammer clicked on empty, he ejected the clip and dropped it into the grave. As he scrambled down the trail he put in a fresh clip and jacked a shell into the chamber.

It was nearly a hundred yards down, and the trail was winding. The car was to the left as he hit the bottom. He could see the woman clearly in the driver's seat. A cigarette was in her left hand. She jabbed the cigarette in and out of her lips as she drummed on the steering wheel with the fingers of her right hand.

Carter hunched down in the coat as much as he could, and walked directly for the car. Again he held the Luger in his right hand just behind his hip.

Closer and closer he came.

Just then, a sliver of moon peeked from behind the clouds. It streamed down, white across the windshield.

"Tilkoff, have you finished? Do you have it?"

Carter kept his eyes on her face, on her eyes in the moonlight. Her lips were a tight slash of red with a rim of white around them.

She was beautiful.

He wondered how such a beautiful person on the outside could be so rotten on the inside.

And then she knew.

She hit the starter and first gear at the same time. The engine roared and the car bucked forward, its rear wheels spinning on the soft, dusty track.

Just as the wheels caught, Carter fired. The slug hit the windshield, shattering it.

But he had seen her duck, and knew that he'd missed.

He leaped to the side among the rocks and, as the car sped past, emptied the clip into the rest of the windows.

Unable to see, she lost control at the curve. The right fender hit the sheer rock, sending the car careening to the left.

When it hit a tree full on, Carter was already running for it, jamming his last full clip into the Luger's butt.

He was still thirty yards away when Anya rolled out the passenger side.

The Killmaster saw two things at the same time: her battered, bloody face where it had collided with the steering wheel or the shattered windshield, and the automatic in her hand.

She fired twice just as Carter rolled to his right into the dirt. The slugs screamed off the rock wall behind him, and he got off one shot that went wild before she was up and running.

Neither of them said a word. There was no need for words.

At the last minute, sitting in the car, she had seen Carter's face beneath the hat brim.

She knew that he meant to kill her.

Carter ran after her. She was heading toward the river. There was no use trying another shot. There were too many rocks and trees, and she constantly darted behind them as she ran.

Then she was gone momentarily. Carter heard the rushing water, then saw the river. The moon was completely out from behind the clouds now. He slowed.

There was no sound, but he sensed that she was just ahead of him, very near.

Then he saw her.

"It's over, Anya."

She turned and looked directly at Carter.

She was standing on the riverbank, grasping a low waving branch. Other leafy branches tumbled over her shoulders as she half crouched, watching first Carter, then the rushing waters below.

"It's no good," Carter hissed. "You wouldn't get a hundred yards in that current."

Her hand came up from her side, holding the gun. Her green eyes were filled with fear, and they fastened on the Luger in Carter's hand.

"I should have killed you," she rasped. Her voice was a hoarse whisper, and there was something of bright satisfaction in it, of oddly unpleasant, wild relief.

"Shoot, Anya," Carter said. "Because, if you don't, I will."

She fired, and the slug ripped bark from a tree just above Carter's shoulder.

The Luger made a soft popping sound in his own hand, and she fell to her knees.

She had both hands on the gun pressed to the spreading crimson stain.

She looked up, her eyes wide. "You did it," she said through sagging lips.

With an effort, she tried to raise the gun.

It was useless.

"Good-bye, Major," Carter said, and fired twice more."

Carter was patting the ground solid over the grave when Luis Estabel climbed the hill and joined him.

"It is a pleasant night."

"It is now," Carter said, dropping the shovel. "Did anyone hear the shots?"

"Perhaps," the young man shrugged. "No matter."

"The car?" Carter asked.

"In the river. It will never be found. You will go now?"

"Yes."

Carter took a folded slip of paper from his pocket and handed it to Estabel. On it was a crude map showing the way from Palermo up into the hills, and a small house with a garden in the rear.

"She lives under the name of Sophia Stillati. I think you can tell her much better than I."

Estabel pocketed the paper without speaking. He opened his arms, and the two men embraced.

"Will we ever see you again?" the young man murmured.

"No," Carter said. "It's better. All the dead can rest in peace now, and the living can get on with living."

"Go with God, my friend."

"Would that I could, Luís. Would that I could."

He walked down the hill and found his car. Across the plaza, he parked and climbed up the long flight of stone steps and through the gates.

It wasn't really necessary, but he wanted one more look.

It was almost dawn now, with the grayness giving the stones an eerie yet somehow peaceful glow.

He didn't stay long, a moment at most. And on the way back, a stooped, black-clad figure stepped from the shadows of the trees to block his way.

"Señor . . ."

"Señora Galadin."

Her gnarled hands tugged at his face as she lifted her frail body to her toes.

"Gracias, señor. Muchas gracias."

She kissed him on both cheeks, and, without another word, turned and faded back into the shadows.

DON'T MISS THE NEXT NEW
NICK CARTER SPY THRILLER

Dragonfire

Captain Chomo was seated behind his desk. He looked up, a big smile on his face, as Carter closed the door and leaned back against it, apparently too weary to move any farther.

"Are you all right?" Chomo asked, his expression now one of concern.

"A little weak . . ." Carter said softly, and he started to sag.

Chomo hurried around his desk toward him. At the last moment, Carter fell into the captain's arms, and as Chomo tried to hold him up, Carter reached out with his right hand and clamped his fingers around Chomo's throat, cutting off the man's air and crushing his windpipe, Chomo's eyes bulging out of their sockets. For just a few seconds as Chomo's struggles weakened, Carter remembered the man seated behind the window, his finger on the button that had sent the electric shocks through his body. Then Chomo's eyes fluttered and rolled back into his head, and his body went limp.

Carter eased the body to the floor and then stepped back, waiting for the sounds of an alarm to be raised. But there was nothing. Chomo was dead, there was no doubt of it. His throat was crushed. He had bitten through his tongue, and blood covered his mouth and dripped down his chin. Carter felt no remorse. By his own admission, Chomo had tortured a lot of men. It was his job.

Moving quickly now, Carter went around to Chomo's desk. The drawers were locked. Straightening out a paper clip, Carter had the locks picked in less than ten seconds. He found his weapons in the bottom drawer: his Luger with extra ammunition and silencer, his stiletto, and his gas bomb. He also found his wallet and money and passport and other personal effects.

It took him another five minutes to make a quick but thorough search of the office. His attaché case wasn't there; but it didn't really matter. There was no possible way of opening it without destroying the contents, and killing whoever was within twenty feet of it.

Carter was a lot weaker from his ordeal than he wanted to admit, but he couldn't let that slow him down. Another twenty-four hours and he would have been incapable of any plan of action.

He listened at the door for a moment or two, but there were no sounds from outside, and he eased it open. The corridor was empty. From the back of the house he could still hear the voices of the guards at dinner.

He strapped on his stiletto, then loaded his Luger, screwing the squat silencer cylinder on the end of the short barrel and pocketing the extra clip of ammunition.

He slipped out into the corridor and raced down to the far end to the dining room door. Keying the ten-second trigger on the gas bomb, he waited a full eight seconds, then opened the door, tossed the bomb inside onto the table around which sat at least a dozen uniformed men, and closed the door again. Someone cried out, but then suddenly the room fell silent.

Without waiting to see what had happened inside—he knew what the scene would look like—he raced back down the corridor to the stairhall.

A guard was just coming in the door. Carter raised his Luger and fired once, the silenced shot making a dull *pop*, destroying the front of the soldier's head.

"Nicholas!" a woman cried from the head of the stairs.

Carter looked up as Tsien-Tsien raced down the stairs toward him. He stepped back and raised his pistol, but he held his fire.

"What have you done? Guards! Guards!" she screamed.

"They're dead," Carter snapped. "Go back upstairs. I don't want to kill you."

"Where are you going?" she rasped.

"Home," Carter replied.

She attacked. Carter managed to sidestep one blow, but then she was on him, a karate chop to his right arm, his hand suddenly going numb, the Luger clattering to the floor.

He managed to shove her away with his shoulder, but she came back at him like a madwoman.

Carter stepped back and hit her with a left hook to her jaw, her head snapping back, blood erupting from her shattered jaw and nose, and she went down, her head bouncing on the tiled floor.

"Christ," Carter muttered.

He scooped up his Luger, checked to make certain

that Tsien-Tsien wasn't dead, and then turned on his heel and raced out the door into the night.

He suspected there would be other guards outside; but so far no alarm had been raised. It had happened too fast for them.

Around back, he found the telephone wires for the house and cut them. If they had radio communications with Kunming, it was a wasted effort, but it might slow them down.

Reaching the two Mercedeses and the VW mini-bus, he put a shot into each gas tank, the vehicles going up with a loud roar, flames shooting a hundred feet into the sky.

He raced back to the corral, where he opened the gate and scattered the horses, then headed back to the front.

A single guard was racing up from the boat dock. Carter fired off a shot on the run, hitting the man in the chest and knocking him off into the water.

A second guard was just climbing out of the boat when Carter hit the dock. The soldier managed to get off one short burst when Carter fired, knocking him back into the boat.

The keys were in the boat's ignition. Carter jumped aboard, heaved the dead guard's body over into the water, cut the lines with his stiletto, and started the engine with a roar. Without waiting for it to warm up, he took off away from the dock across the dark water, behind him flames still rising up into the night sky from the burning automobiles, the back of the house starting to catch fire.

—From DRAGONFIRE
A New Nick Carter Spy Thriller
From Jove in February 1988

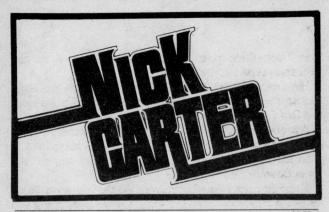

☐	0-441-57290-1	**CROSSFIRE RED**	$2.75
☐	0-441-57282-0	**THE CYCLOPS CONSPIRACY**	$2.50
☐	0-441-14222-2	**DEATH HAND PLAY**	$2.50
☐	0-515-09055-7	**EAST OF HELL**	$2.75
☐	0-441-21877-6	**THE EXECUTION EXCHANGE**	$2.50
☐	0-441-45520-4	**THE KREMLIN KILL**	$2.50
☐	0-441-24089-5	**LAST FLIGHT TO MOSCOW**	$2.50
☐	0-441-51353-0	**THE MACAO MASSACRE**	$2.50
☐	0-441-52276-9	**THE MAYAN CONNECTION**	$2.50
☐	0-441-52510-5	**MERCENARY MOUNTAIN**	$2.50
☐	0-441-57502-1	**NIGHT OF THE WARHEADS**	$2.50
☐	0-441-58612-0	**THE NORMANDY CODE**	$2.50
☐	0-441-69180-3	**PURSUIT OF THE EAGLE**	$2.50
☐	0-441-57287-1	**SLAUGHTER DAY**	$2.50
☐	0-441-79831-4	**THE TARLOV CIPHER**	$2.50
☐	0-441-57285-5	**TERROR TIMES TWO**	$2.50
☐	0-441-57283-9	**TUNNEL FOR TRAITORS**	$2.50
☐	0-515-09112-X	**KILLING GAMES**	$2.75
☐	0-515-09214-2	**TERMS OF VENGEANCE**	$2.75
☐	0-515-09168-5	**PRESSURE POINT**	$2.75
☐	0-515-09255-X	**NIGHT OF THE CONDOR**	$2.75
☐	0-515-09324-6	**THE POSEIDON TARGET**	$2.75
☐	0-515-09376-9	**THE ANDROPOV FILE**	$2.75
☐	0-515-09444-7	**DRAGONFIRE**	$2.75
☐	0-515-09490-0	**BLOODTRAIL TO MECCA** (on sale March '88)	$2.75
☐	0-515-09519-2	**DEATHSTRIKE** (on sale April '88)	$2.75

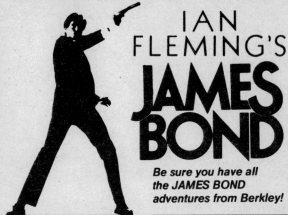